Safe
with you

a goldheart novella

JENNY BUNTING

Editing: Lopt & Cropt Editing

Proofreading: Horus Proofreading

Cover and Illustration: Julie Olivia

For all the folks who panic when they don't have easy access to a restroom.

This is for you.

BOOKS BY JENNY BUNTING

Here in Lillyvale

Happiness (Caroline and Brady)

Here (Zoey and Jonathan)

Hustle (Taylor and Malcolm)

Home (Addison and Kirk)

Hubby (Makenna and Dan)

Stuck in Love

Please Be Seated (Erin and Landon)

In Case of Emergency (Cassie and Smith)

For Your Safety (Raegan and Henry)

Finch Family

Fool's Gold (Annie and Cameron)

Gold Rush (Whitney and Reid)

Standalones

Safe with You (Izzie and Eugene "Thumper")

A NOTE FROM JENNY

Thank you for picking up *Safe with You*! I hope you enjoy it.

While this novella is light in tone, it does begin with an armed robbery and imprisonment of the hero and heroine. No one is harmed in the novella. If you are sensitive, please take care of yourself.

1

EUGENE

"It must be payday," Mike Larson says, as I step onto the curb in front of the Goldheart Credit Union. Mike is a good guy I fish with sometimes; I always say hi to him when I see him out and about.

"It sure is," I say, holding up my wallet. The edges of my paycheck stick out from my billfold.

"You're the only guy I know who still gets a paper check."

"I like to keep it old school. Direct deposit is for suckers."

Mike chuckles. "Whatever you say."

We chat for a little while, mostly about fishing. Everywhere I go, I see someone I know. I feel like goddamn Goldheart royalty every time I leave my house.

"Good to see you. Make sure to say hi to your parents for me."

"Sure will," I say, shaking his hand as I walk through the door of the bank.

No line. Perfect.

Ms. Keller is invested in a romance novel as usual.

"Good afternoon, my lovely bank teller."

She always jumps three feet out of her chair in surprise and today is no different.

"Oh Eugene, what a pleasure."

"The pleasure is all mine," I say. She presents her hand and I kiss it, like I do every other Friday.

She's pretty much the only person who calls me by my real name. I'm thirty-three years old with the name of an old coot. It was my grandpa's name and my parents didn't know what to name me, so I got Eugene. In high school, my friends started calling me Thumper, and it stuck. Now, it's fifty-fifty I turn my head when someone yells "Eugene" at me.

Grandpa Gene doesn't even call me Eugene.

"Have you gotten to the naughty bits yet?" I ask. Yes, I flirt with sixty-year-old women.

"Not yet," she says, setting the splayed book down on her counter. "We've been busier than usual."

I look around at the empty lobby.

"Not now," she says. "Did you get paid today?"

"Yes, ma'am," I say, pulling out the paper check. It has dirt smudges since I got it at the end of my shift with the construction crew I'm a part of.

I turn it over and endorse the back with my signature.

"Do you want to finally open an account, Eugene?" she asks.

She asks me every time. I don't trust banks. I like to see my money, and I like to pay for everything in cash. Bea at the

Goldheart Market sees me more often since I use Western Union and money orders more than my hairbrush. "Not today, ma'am," I say.

"Suit yourself." She turns the check over to stamp it and then pulls out a blank deposit form. I sense movement behind me, so I turn my head.

Isabella St. Clair.

The editor of our *Goldheart Gazette*. Brains and beauty to the nines.

I love a tall woman, and she's only a couple inches shorter than I am. Long legs, long, silky blonde hair. Enough tenacity to fill Main Street. She's holding an almost empty iced coffee close to her chest, like she keeps her cards.

From what I've heard about her, she hasn't made any friends; she just works her tail off. I'm the friendliest guy in Goldheart, and although I've seen her around, I've never had a full conversation with her. From her reputation around town, she's a damn good reporter, although she looks visibly bored at the Little League games she has to cover.

"Eugene, sign the form right here," Ms. Keller says, pointing at the deposit slip.

Now comes my favorite part.

She counts out the hundreds, just like I like them. She also counts out the remainder in singles. It might look like I'm going to the strip club, but I just love my wallet to be thick.

I tuck the wad of cash in my wallet and turn around. Isabella stares at me with contempt. "Ma'am," I say, tipping my ballcap to her. Isabella crosses her arms and mutters a greeting back. Not sure what she's heard about me, but her reaction means it can't be good.

I have a reputation as a player that I didn't really earn. It's mostly because of my buddy, Cameron.

Cameron got around like the town bicycle for years until he started dating Annie, a woman who is way too good for him. I've been with my fair share of women, but I've never had bad intentions with them. I go into every encounter wanting it to last, wanting what my parents have.

It just never goes that way.

The Swift, my favorite place in Goldheart, isn't the same without Cameron these days, now that he's basically shacked up with Annie. It used to be good times with him, nights full of drinking and bullshitting. Now, it's just the sad regulars and me when I go—Pete crying over his ex and Winston getting too drunk and needing the one Uber driver in town to pick his sorry ass up. I've driven him home a time or two myself.

When I don't go to the Swift, I don't meet women. When I don't meet women, I can't make love to them.

It's been a couple months for me, and Big Thump is getting restless.

Big Thump is my dick.

Lately, I've been drinking alone on my porch with my puppy, Bambi. She's the woman who's stuck around the longest. She licks me constantly, but it's not the same as a human female doing it.

Maybe I can meet a woman at a respectable place.

Like a financial institution.

I hold out my hand to Isabella. "I don't think we've formally met. Eugene Walker, but my friends call me Thumper," I say.

She looks at my hand and back up, like it's a trick. "Nice try," she says, tucking her iced coffee in her armpit so she can cross her arms. Ms. Keller watches instead of calling Isabella up to the window.

"Excuse me?" I ask.

"Women have warned me about you," Isabella says. "That anything out of your mouth is sweet-talking to get me under you."

While I'm appalled at the current state of my reputation amongst the women of this town, there *is* an ounce of truth to that, I suppose.

"All I want is you to shake my hand, Isabella."

"Izzie," she says, crossing her arms tighter.

"You don't like your name?"

"*Twilight* became popular when I was in high school, and I had it quoted to me constantly, so yeah, the name carries some baggage for me."

"I feel that. Imagine having the same name as half of the Shady Oak Retirement Home off of Main."

"Huh," she says. "Why do they call you Thumper?"

"Well…" I drawl, winking. She rolls her eyes.

"Come on up here, Isabella," Ms. Keller says. She breezes past me, a whiff of floral perfume drifting off of her. It makes Big Thump jolt. A woman I dated a few months ago smelled like that, but I could forget that woman for Isabella.

I stand in place, contemplating what to do. Do I wait and talk to her more when she's done with her transaction? Try to get her to think differently of me?

Regardless, I could use some complimentary coffee right now.

I slowly pump out the coffee from the carafe as I watch Izzie talk with Ms. Keller, who is speaking softly.

Izzie looks back, her eyes narrowed at me.

"What are you still doing here?"

"Getting some coffee."

"Are you sure?"

I hold up the paper cup. "Best coffee in the town." I take a sip and shudder. It's cold, and I think I got a tablespoon of grounds. I still smile, but I'm starting to sweat.

"Eugene, honey, that coffee is old. Do you want me to make you some more?" Ms. Keller asks.

"No, it's fine," I reply, my voice raspy. I have been traumatized, but I take another sip.

Izzie looks back again.

"I'm just gonna enjoy this coffee right here," I say as I lean against the wall.

Ms. Keller has a smirk on her fuchsia-colored lips. "Isabella, Eugene is a good boy."

"I'm like a golden retriever, I'm such a good boy," I say.

"You know, Eugene is quite the catch," Ms. Keller tells her.

"I'm not available right now," Izzie says to Ms. Keller.

Damn, does she have a boyfriend? Maybe I *should* leave. Ms. Keller beats me to it.

"Do you have a boyfriend, dear?"

"No," she says. "Just focusing on myself."

"Well, can I at least walk you to your car?" I ask her.

"It's three in the afternoon," she says.

"There might be turkeys."

"They are getting more and more brazen," Ms. Keller says. "You should let him walk you to your car, honey. Eugene has experience with birds."

You fight *one* ostrich, and people won't ever let you live that down.

Izzie thanks Ms. Keller and walks away, but her wallet flies from her arms in her rush, and lands halfway between me and her.

The door opens behind us as I pick up her wallet to hand it to her.

A human-size chicken rushes in with a shotgun.

It wasn't turkeys we had to be worried about, after all. It was a goddamn chicken.

"What the fu—" I yell, my mouth down to my nipples.

A female voice says, "Folks, this is a robbery. Please stay calm and do not make any sudden movements."

I raise my hands. No need to spook a chicken with a gun. Calm rushes over me, since this isn't the first time I've had a gun on me. Growing up with the feral children of Goldheart, a BB gun has been pointed at my crotch more than once and I was the victim of one terrifying mugging in San Francisco. I can't say you get used to it, but the sight isn't a shock to me.

Izzie turns around, white as milk, her lips parted in shock. I want to comfort her and tell her not to worry. I won't let her die by the hands of a shotgun-wielding chicken. However, I'm not totally confident I can promise that. Who knows how crazy a criminal has to be to wear a costume that looks like Big Bird's methed-out cousin?

The costume has seen better days, with flaky yellow feathers and dirty orange legs to white tennis shoes. I don't watch the news, but I wonder if this chicken has robbed other banks, not just this one.

Do I run? Do I tackle a chicken?

"Oh my God," Izzie whispers.

I hold out my hand to signal no sudden movements, when the chicken moseys up to the teller. Ms. Keller is as calm as you can expect.

She wails.

"Ms. Keller, it's going to be okay," I say. "Just do what the fowl says."

"Shut the fuck up, Thumper," the chicken yells.

Oh shit, this poultry knows me. How, I don't know.

What if I fucked this chicken?

Izzie takes small, measured steps back toward me, and I creep toward her. I will throw her behind me if I have to. She's too pretty and talented to die in a bank robbery. I can die, no problem. She can write a news story about me. I wonder what picture she'll use.

I hope it's my 4H photo with my favorite goat, Gilda.

"Do something," Izzie hisses at me.

"What the fuck you want me to do?" I hiss back.

Tears well in her eyes as we stand frozen, watching a sobbing Ms. Keller take stacks of cash from her till and load up the pillowcase that the chicken gave her. The pillowcase is light purple with rainbows and unicorns on it, definitely a child's pillowcase.

Which single moms have I dated?

Allie, Julie, Elsie…

The chicken doesn't sound like any of them.

"You two," the chicken says, shotgun in one hand, pillowcase in the other. "Into the vault."

"What about me, chicken ma'am?" Ms. Keller says.

"No, just you two," the chicken says to us.

"You can't be serious," I yell, my hands still up.

"Do I look serious?" the chicken asks.

"Well, you're wearing a chicken costume. Draw your own conclusions."

"Get your smart ass in the vault, Thumper," the chicken says.

"Don't you hurt Ms. Keller, okay?" I ask, walking toward the vault. Izzie shivers next to me, a tear slipping from her cheek. "And please don't hurt this fine woman."

The chicken stops, holding the shotgun toward us. Did I tap into the chicken's empathy? What is going on in that small brain?

"I won't," the chicken says, its feathered shoulders dropped. "It's just something I have to do. So you don't get out."

"Understood. Come on, Izzie," I say, offering my hand. She takes it without complaint. Her hand is soft and warm in mine.

Ms. Keller punches a series of numbers into the keypad to open the vault. The deadbolt disengaging clangs like a jail cell.

"There's no money in there, chicken ma'am," Ms. Keller says. "I don't have the keys for the safety deposit boxes…"

The chicken hesitates, but then waves us in. "That's fine. Get in. Now."

Izzie and I walk into the vault. We stand there, our hands still clasped together, as we watch the chicken and Ms. Keller close the door on us.

Ms. Keller whispers something as she closes the door.

It's so damn quiet in here.

Until I hear a sob.

Turning my head, I see Izzie hunched over, her body convulsing as she cries. Rushing to her, I take her in my arms, pressing her against my flannel shirt. She hiccups against my chest as her sobs morph into whimpers.

"It's okay, Izzie. You're safe here with me," I say. Her hair is as soft as it looks as I push the tiny hairs away from her face.

I don't know if it's her in my arms or what. I just know that I will protect her at all costs.

"Safe," she repeats and then giggles. "Safe, like a bank safe."

"Sure," I say, rubbing her back. "You're safe with me in a safe."

She pulls away and looks up at me with large blue eyes. "You promise?"

"I promise. No matter what happens, I won't let the chicken hurt you."

"Thanks, Thumper," she says as she continues to cry softly into my chest.

I should be upset too, but I'm not.

If I survive this, this will be a wild story to tell for years to come while I sip my beloved Budweiser at barbecues. If I die, I've had a good life. When the good Lord calls me home, I'll come running.

I just hope Izzie isn't scarred by this. This was meant to happen for some reason.

I just don't know what the reason is yet.

2

IZZIE

This is how I'm going to die.

Stuck in a bank vault with Thumper, the town sweet-talker, after being forced in by a woman wearing a chicken costume. And I can't even do my job properly. My notebook is tucked in my purse—the purse that I left in my car with my phone.

I just read an article about how phones are ruling our lives, and now I have no way to take notes the *one* time I'm in a bank robbery.

I'm the worst reporter ever.

Goldheart is a cute, idyllic little town with no violent crime, ever, so I let my guard down, and now I'm suffering the consequences. It's what happens when you cover this town's "news." Or lack thereof.

When the front-page story of their paper is how ducks crossing the road is holding up traffic, you start to think the town doesn't have a dark side. You get complacent. You forget all of your crisis training, just in time for a woman dressed up as a chicken to hold up the bank while you're getting cash.

I moved to Goldheart six months ago to accept an editor position at their three-times-weekly paper, the *Goldheart Gazette*. Bright-eyed and full of hope, I wanted to report the news and establish myself in the town to gain enough experience so that I can apply in a bigger market after I had a full year under my belt. Work my way up to telling the stories I want to.

Uncovering secrets. Debunking lies. I dream big. I want the accolades, the awards. I want a Pulitzer. I want a Peabody.

Constant peril would be my destiny when I became a war journalist or covered crimes and high-profile cases. That was for the future, though. In Goldheart, I was never supposed to have a gun pointed at me, or be part of anything traumatic. I thought I had time to prepare for trouble, but trouble found me instead.

I'd been blessed with a nice childhood and a stress-free adolescence. Even my divorce from my high school sweetheart was pleasant—ended through a mediator, and we agreed on everything. Our marriage evaporated like our love for each other did three years in.

I grew up in Lillyvale, a suburb outside of Sacramento and about forty-five minutes from Goldheart, if you haul ass. Goldheart is a smaller version of my hometown, with a picture-perfect main street and friendly but gossipy locals. In the six months I've been here, I've been on the hunt for a story, any story, that would scratch that itch. Underground gambling operation? A drug runner laundering money through Betty's Café? An unsolved murder of a teenage girl?

Nothing. This town is as clean as a Hallmark movie.

Life was turning into one boring, Groundhog Day-esque loop. Little League game. Board meeting. A fun run.

All wholesome, angst-free stories.

Until I was blindsided by a shotgun-holding chicken.

How ironic life can be.

Now, I'm stuck in here with a grown man named Thumper.

The minute I heard the nickname Thumper, I knew exactly who he was. When I saw the cowboy boots and the belt buckle, I knew more. He opened his mouth and immediately began flirting, and it was confirmed. I may be naïve, but I'm not an idiot.

A man like Thumper is only interested in what's between my legs, not what's in my heart or my brain. A man like Thumper would be intimidated by me, my tall stature, my opinions, and my ambition.

However, the minute his strong arms comforted me inside the bank vault, I turned into a helpless woman whose feminism evaporates at the first sign of inconvenience.

"It's okay, Izzie. I don't hear anything out there," Thumper says, rocking me in his lap. I wipe my eyes and breathe in, the snot rattling in my nose. How am I going to handle the tough stories if I cry after being imprisoned in a small-town bank vault by a chicken?

"Why did this happen?"

"Not sure," Thumper says. "It seems fucked up to say, but maybe I was meant to be here with you. This will be an experience to remember, for sure."

Tears disappear from my eyes at his words. He probably

doesn't mean anything by it, but it sounded romantic, nonetheless.

Maybe he's just being nice.

"Let me try the door. Maybe Ms. Keller left it ajar so we could get out," Thumper says, standing up, leaving me slouched on the hard floor. I wipe the wetness from my cheeks as I watch him try the door handle. Nothing. He looks around the door, probably for a keypad or buzzer, but he finds nothing.

"Well, shit," he says. "That would've been too easy."

"I don't have my phone," I tell him.

"I have mine." Thumper pulls out an ancient Nokia and flips it open. I can see the shine of the duct tape from here. How does he even function with that fossil? The whole reason I started reading articles about minimizing my digital use is I've been horrified by the amount of screen time I was accruing lately. That's what happens when you live in a town when you know next to no one.

You spend a lot of time on TikTok.

Last night, I read article after article about leaving your phone where you can't access it when I was a bottle of wine deep.

Today was the first day I decided to spend some time without it.

The first time I leave my phone behind, and look what happened.

Thumper studies his screen. "No service in here. Damn."

"Maybe if you had a newer phone."

He shakes his phone at me. "This works just fine. My parents and my employer can get hold of me, and the best part? No texting."

"You don't *text*?" I would die if I had to talk to someone over the phone every time I had to get hold of them. I'm a text-message-and-email girl all the way. I only call because it's part of my job. All other phone calls are relegated to the written word.

"No. Too impersonal. I like face-to-face."

Who is this man?

Thumper walks around the room, holding up the phone, looking for bars. He punches 911 over and over, hitting the send button, waiting for something to click. I watch him for ten minutes, determined to find some weak cellular wave that could communicate with his relic.

"Technology can suck my balls," Thumper says, snapping the phone closed again.

"You hate it?"

"With a fiery, burning passion. I avoid it as much as possible. Don't trust it."

Instead of being terrified, I'm intrigued. I read about people who refuse technology in the article, and now I'm in front of someone who despises it.

"Do you have a TV?" I ask.

He shakes his head.

"A laptop?"

"I do have that," he says. "I barely use it, though."

"Do you have an email?" I ask. Anything to keep my mind off

the thought that I might die in here.

He squints to think. "I do, but I haven't checked it in two months. It's all junk anyway. I do have a cheap fax machine in my kitchen."

Who is this man?

I'd be less shocked if he told me he's wrestled an alligator. At least the shock has dried my tears and made me focus on the audacity of Thumper refusing to participate in technology and the modern world. And being the only man on earth who works construction and owns a *fax machine*. That he keeps in his kitchen next to his toaster.

If he even owns a toaster.

If I wasn't so appalled, I would be impressed.

Thumper closes his phone and rests his hands on his belt. I haven't seen him up close before. He's a little taller than I am, with broad shoulders stretching his flannel, and tight jeans curving around his ass. He's in good shape. I can see why the ladies love him.

Even his belt buckle is cool. I can't make out the detail from here, but it sure is shiny and gold.

His dark blond hair peaks out from under his dirty baseball cap with a name I can't read, it's so faded. His skin is red, probably from working outside, but he's got kind eyes.

I can see why girls would give him a chance. He's not bad-looking. The personality does give him a couple extra points.

"Hot damn," he says, spotting something behind me. A coat, a purse, and a separate cloth bag hang on a hook by the door, presumably Ms. Keller's. She must think it's safer in here. "Do you think there's a phone in there?"

"Let's check."

Going through Ms. Keller's purse seems wrong, like it's a violation of privacy. I don't want to be here forever, but I also don't want to be the person going through an older woman's purse.

Thumper points to it. "No disrespect, Izzie, but you're the lady. It would be more polite for you to go through it."

"Is this ethical?"

"Do you want to get out of here or not?" Thumper asks.

I huff out a breath, going against every moral and respect I have for nice, older women, and take the purse off of the hook. It's a generic faux leather purse, stuffed with items. I unzip it, and the first thing I pull out is a thick maxi pad, thicker than the book I'm currently reading on my nightstand.

"What *is* that?" Thumper asks. Once he realizes what it is, he looks at it in horror, like I just held up a used tampon. He walks away, hacking.

"Are you dry-heaving?"

He points at the purse, coughing.

"It's unused. Get it together."

"Keep looking," he says, his voice hoarse as he covers his mouth.

I stick my hand in again, feeling a gum package, keys, a wallet, lots of pens, and finally, a phone.

I expected a Jitterbug or a phone like Thumper's. Instead, it's a gleaming, shiny iPhone. Steve Jobs looks down on us and smiles.

I tap the screen to illuminate it. Notifications overpower the home screen.

I click the side button to bring up the passcode screen and tap Emergency. There's one bar in the upper right corner.

There's a tiny glimmer of hope I will not die in here.

I type 911, and my heart stops when it does not ring right away. Thumper has gotten over his maxi pad sighting and watches me.

"Nine-one-one, what is your emergency?"

"Hi, yes, this is Izzie St. Clair. Thumper Walker and I were witnesses to a bank robbery at the Goldheart Credit Union. The suspect was wearing a chicken costume. We're currently stuck in the safety deposit box room."

I heard a pause and the hint of a chuckle. I'm embarrassed that the one time I was a witness to a robbery, a chicken costume was involved.

"Okay, are either of you injured?"

"No," I say. "We're just locked in here."

The operator types and asks me questions. When the call is wrapping up, she asks, "Is this a good number to call you at?"

"Yes," I say.

"Hang tight," she says. "We will call you back once we have more info."

"Thank you," I say. I end the call, and a smile erupts on my face.

"This is great!" I yell as I collide with Thumper, hugging him around his barrel chest. He picks me up, and I wrap my legs around his waist in excitement as I bounce on his stomach. It's the most intimate thing I've done with a man lately, but I'm so excited, I couldn't help but tackle him.

I pull my face away, and our gaze crashes. My smile drops, because his eyelids are dropped halfway down his light eyes, looking at me like I'm a pack of fresh Oreos. He rubs his lips together, and I wonder if he will kiss me.

I slide down his body, walking away, breaking the moment.

"Now, we wait," I say, crossing my arms.

Thumper crosses his arms too, tucking his hands into his elbows. "How do you want to pass the time?"

I look at the purse and look back at him. "Do you think there's a notepad in there? I want to write down some of what happened, so I don't forget when I write this up for the paper."

"Look."

"It feels weird," I say, although I'd already been elbow-deep in it looking for the phone.

"You could use mine," Thumper says, pulling out a mini-notebook and a pen. His jeans are definitely too tight to carry things like this, including his bulky cell phone.

"Why do you carry this?"

"I love to take notes." He hands it to me, and I take it with two fingers like a germaphobe crab.

I flip it to a fresh page and begin scrawling quotes. I look around to describe the room we're stuck in, filling page after page with details. I don't realize Thumper is studying me.

"What?" I ask when I look up and catch him staring.

He sits back on his elbows. "It's just interesting, is all. You're really pretty when you're concentrating. Well, you're pretty all the time."

"Pretty" is not something I'm called often. I never get catcalled, hit on. I married the first man I ever slept with—and look how well that turned out.

"You say that to all the girls."

"Just the pretty ones."

I roll my eyes, and he chuckles to himself. It's deep and throaty, and I don't know why my stomach is swirling.

It's been about three years since I've had sex. That must be it.

Ms. Keller's phone rings, and I jump. It fumbles in my hand before I answer it.

"Hello?"

"Is this Izzie?" a male voice asks.

"Yes," I say.

"This is Officer Lance Compton. The police force is in pursuit of the suspect, and the suspect caused two car accidents, so we will be there as soon as we can."

"What about Ms. Keller?"

"The robber dropped Ms. Keller off on the outskirts of town. She's alright."

I breathe out a sigh of relief.

"How long will we be in here?"

"I'm not sure, Izzie. We will get you out as soon as we can."

"Who is it?" Thumper whispers, pointing at the phone.

"Lance Compton."

"Give it to me," Thumper says, bending his fingers to ask for the phone.

I hand it over.

"What's up, sweetums?"

My mouth drops. I've never talked to an authority figure like that. Ever.

"Respectfully, Lance, I see how often you and your officers get coffee. You can't spare one officer to get over here and let us out?"

Thumper nods as he listens.

"Whatever. You owe me a beer. No, wait, two beers. Make it snappy. Later, sweetums."

Thumper takes the phone from his ear and hands it to me. He definitely notices the look of horror on my face.

"What?"

"You called a police officer 'sweetums'."

"Yes. He's a buddy of mine. Lance is a good guy. We get a beer together a lot."

"Why 'sweetums'?"

"His wife called him that once in public, and we have never, ever let him live it down," Thumper says. "Lance has no idea when we'll get out of here. It might be a while. A few hours."

"A few *hours*?" I ask.

"You're not dealing with the most experienced cops. They mostly deal with noise complaints and the occasional loose dog. A thieving chicken is the most excitement this police force has seen in ten years."

"Oh," I say. I stare at my notes, making notes here and there. I suppose being stuck in here with Thumper Walker is not a terrible way to spend a few hours. He seems much sweeter and more genuine than the reputation he's got. Knowing the chicken left the scene makes me feel better.

"So, since we'll be in here a while, tell me your story, Izzie," Thumper says, clasping his fingers together.

My pen pauses above my paper. "There's not much to tell."

"Sure there is. You're the editor of our fine periodical. You must have some doozies of stories."

I think for a moment, flipping through my notes.

"Did you get everything for this story? About the chicken?"

"I think so."

My heart rate has finally slowed. The chicken costume flashes through my thoughts, and I cringe. At least chickens will replace my recurring nightmare of falling off a non-descript building.

Somehow, I don't feel that bothered by a chicken pointing a shotgun in my face anymore. Going through it with Thumper made it not a big deal.

I can't explain it, but it feels like nothing bad could happen if I were with Thumper.

"Do you think I'll ever be able to eat chicken again?" I ask.

Thumper laughs, and there is the stomach churning again. "What?"

"Chicken. I wonder if this will give me nightmares later. I mean, I'm fine right now, but the PTSD hasn't kicked in yet."

"It's too ridiculous for nightmares," Thumper says. "I mean, I do have a recurring nightmare of being late for work."

"Everyone has those nightmares."

"True, but does a giant squid ever block your car from leaving your house?"

"What?" My mouth drops like Oprah hearing a guest's bombshell.

Thumper nods. "I wish I was making it up. That squid has been terrorizing me for years. It's why I refuse to try that shit at sushi."

He eats sushi? That's not something I would have guessed about him.

"What's the best place to get sushi in Goldheart?"

"Juno Sushi. The best."

I've been busy for the six months I've been here, even if it was only transposing the police logs of equipment theft and reporting on a minor drug bust here and there. I've made one good friend, Tara, who owns Gold Roast, the best coffee shop in Goldheart, but we usually hang out on her deck and drink wine.

"I haven't heard of that one."

"I'll take you there sometime."

"On a date?"

"If you'd like. Or a celebration of getting out of here. Surviving the Great Chicken Bank Run."

It would be nice to try a place I haven't tried yet. I'm tempted.

"I'll let you know," I say. I look down at Thumper's notebook pad. "Care to give a quote about your experience?"

"Sure," Thumper says, clearing his throat. "I had the pleasure of being stuck with Ms. St. Clair, and I have to say, I've never had a more pleasant experience being robbed."

I stare him down like an exasperated high school history teacher.

"What? It's the truth."

"This is not about me. It's about our experience."

"This is our experience. I'm stuck with you." Thumper lies down on the cold floor of the vault, stretching his arms over his head. "I highly recommend this. It feels surprisingly good on the back."

I pause before I set the notebook to the side and lie down as well. The "I'm stuck with you" sounds like a hardship for Thumper, who just called me pretty. Now I'm lying on the floor of a bank vault, like Noah and Allie did in the intersection in *The Notebook*.

My mind is too racy for this kind of meditation.

"Officer Compton said Ms. Keller is okay. The chicken dropped her off on the outskirts of town."

"That's a relief. Ms. Keller is too pure for this world."

"When do you think we will be rescued?" I ask. I can't let

myself speculate without an outside influence. My ex-husband often told me "You think too much."

"Soon, I guess. They'll want to get us out as soon as possible. It'll be nice to see the police when they're rescuing me, rather than when I'm in trouble."

My face feels tingly at the admission. "What?"

"I've been in the back of a cop car once or twice. Actually, four times."

"You must be wild."

Thumper laughs again. My god, why does my stomach feel so fluttery? It's just a laugh. A deep, full-of-joy laugh, but still. "I've had my own share of fun."

"Like what?"

"Well…*allegedly*, I stole a naked statue from Victor Wisteria's front lawn."

"The millionaire?" I've spoken to him a couple times on the phone, when he requested a profile on himself for the paper. He sounds pompous and exactly the kind of person who would have a marble statue on his front lawn in a rural community with no chain stores.

"The very one. He's a prick. That's off-the-record."

Off-the-record. Smart.

"Anyway, he was a dick to one of my friends, and the statue is completely ridiculous so we *may* have stolen it to fuck with him. We *may* have wanted to dress it up in a Hawaiian shirt and sunglasses and put it back the next day. However, the motherfucker found out and called the police. My friends didn't get nailed, but I took one for the team. I was overnight in jail, but Victor decided not to press charges."

"Did Cameron help you out? *Allegedly?*"

Thumper laughs again. "No comment."

I met Annie, Cameron's girlfriend, on my second day at work, after she called the paper asking for a feature on the nineties prom she was planning with the Finch family, who own the Woody Finch Brewery. I went to take photos for the feature and dressed up in a Fun Dip costume I found online. Not a single man looked at me the entire night. I thought my costume was clever.

Thumper looks at me and makes my insides gooey. "I still want to know more about you."

"There's not much to tell."

"You mentioned you didn't have a boyfriend. Are you seeing anyone? No partner?"

I shake my head. The concrete floor feels good on my back, cool against my flushed skin. Distracts me from my bladder, growing fuller by the minute. "What about you?"

He shakes his head. "I did. Once."

I check my watch. We've been stuck for approximately an hour, and I haven't heard any commotion outside. No telling how long we'll be stuck in here. I'll bite. "What do you mean, 'once'?"

"I was married," Thumper whispers, looking at the ceiling.

"Really? Me too."

"What happened with your person?"

I swallow a lump. The marriage ended with a hug and a promise to keep in touch. Then my best friend floated away, started a new life, and broke his word. The man I trusted more than anyone is now a stranger.

"We were high school sweethearts. We grew up and grew apart." Usually, people look at me with sympathy when I tell them. Thumper's eyes are just kind.

"Similar thing happened to me. I met this girl, and I fell in love. Hard. I married her in the church in front of our friends and family. Two months passed, and she told me she didn't love me anymore. Wanted a divorce."

"Oh," I say. It explains his reputation. "Does she still live here?"

Thumper shakes his head. He focuses on the ceiling. "She moved to the UK. Supposedly she had a pen pal who said he wanted to see her. The promise of him meant more than the reality of me."

My heart drops from my chest to the floor. How heartbreaking. Thumper's light eyes cloud with moisture as he sniffles back.

"You're a big softie, aren't you?" I say, touching his arm. His tiny arm hairs stand on end.

"How can you tell?"

"I am very intuitive."

"That's smart for nosy."

"True," I say. "Comes with the job. I'm paid to be nosy. But you probably know way more business about this town than I will ever know."

"That's true. However, I'm telling you none of it. I've already revealed too much about Victor's statue."

"Fair enough." That's been my experience in this town so far. No one willing to tell me a thing. Treating me like I'm constantly tapped. Looking at me like I'm an outsider. "From what I noticed, this town is a gossip mill. So, what's the secret? How do I work my way into the hearts of this town?"

"Time," he says. "And trust." He finally turns his head toward me. "Can I trust you?"

"Yes," I say, the word vibrating in my throat. The way Thumper protected me, held me while I cried, I know he's a good man.

"Good," Thumper says. "Because my word is strong like steel, darlin'."

I can't help but melt at the term of endearment. Makes me realize how much I miss that kind of affection.

3

EUGENE

I've been trying to talk Big Thump down from an embarrassing boner for ten minutes. We talked about my divorce. We talked about Goldheart. We talked about trust.

And all Big Thump can think about is sex. Damn him.

She *will* notice. My jeans are tight because I once heard ladies like tight jeans on country boys, and I've been enjoying one too many beers lately. And been eating so many goddamn nachos at the Swift.

She's probably into lean guys who read Shakespeare in between lifting barbells. I'm farm-strong—broad and sturdy but lacking chiseled definition. And I don't think I finished a single book in high school.

Smart women usually wise up about me pretty fast and don't give me the time of day after that. I'm not sure if Izzie is naïve or just bored, stuck in here. All I know is I want her. I want her very much. But I know she'll lose all interest in me once she realizes how much of a dumbass I am.

It's more than the hair and the legs now. Her brain fascinates me, and I'm sure she could teach me a thing or two. I might even read a book after this because the next time I meet a woman like Izzie, I'll want a chance with her.

But we both know Izzie wouldn't be talking to me if we weren't stuck here.

"What's the first thing you will do when you get out of here?" I ask.

"Pee," Izzie says, sitting up. "I think I need to stand up."

"Do you need to pee right now?"

She points to her almost empty iced coffee cup. "I'm regretting getting that as a reward for doing my errands today."

She walks the length of the bank vault and turns around, walking the opposite direction. She exhales, and I notice that look of terror all too well.

"You know, my sister had a tiny bladder," I say, trying to soothe her. "We couldn't go forty-five minutes in the car without her having to pee. She could've drunk nothing, and she'd still have to go. My dad thought she was too dramatic, so he tested it constantly. My sister always got a look just like the one on your face."

"And what's that?" Izzie says, a swirl of discomfort and terror in her eyes.

"Like you're scared to death of peeing yourself," I say. "Anyway, we were on this long road trip I don't know where, but Flo…"

"Wait, your sister's name is Flo?" Izzie asks. "That's fitting."

"Short for Florence. She got teased all the time because she was always in the bathroom. Then that damn insurance lady with the red lipstick had the audacity to go by my sister's name," I say. "Anyway, she begged our dad to pull over. I knew when she was serious so I smacked my dad on the shoulder and said, 'If you don't pull over for Flo, I will pee on *you*.' We found a gas station, and my sister kissed me on the head and ran in. I've never seen someone so relieved when she came back out."

"You sound like a good brother."

"I'm a *great* brother. When Flo got married last year, I was her man of honor. I planned an epic bachelorette party. Epic."

"I bet you did." Izzie hunches over. "I have to pee so bad."

When she looks up, I point to her cup sitting on the floor. She shakes her head violently.

"It would be easy," I say.

"For you, maybe. I can't do it. I would get it everywhere, and I can't pee in front of you."

"Why?"

"It would be embarrassing."

"I won't think anything less of you if you pee in the corner of a room into a cup."

She bounces on her sneakers. "How much longer do you think we have, do you think?"

I shrug. "It could be hours. Again, not the brightest cops you will ever find. Just pee in the cup. I'll turn my back, plug my ears, and we will never speak of this again. Never."

Izzie studies the cup, weighing her options. Pain or a little humiliation?

"Be brave," I say. "Pee in the cup."

"Okay," she says, crouching for the cup that still has an inch or so of brown water in the bottom, and walks to the corner. I turn around, staring at the safety deposit box wall. Clothes rustle behind me, and I hear the lid come off and I stick my fingers in my ears. I think about food. What kind of meal I will have after I get out of here? How long we're in here determines what I get. A cheeseburger from the Swift is the bare minimum; if I'm stuck here for two hours, I will get that. Three hours, sushi. More than half a day, I'm driving to a casino and dropping thirty for a buffet.

My fingers hurt my ears, so I take them out and she's still peeing. Izzie pees like she just got defrosted in a cryochamber. A tiny moan leaves her.

I chuckle, covering my mouth.

"Don't laugh!"

"I'm not laughing." Trying not makes it worse, and I'm heaving with silent laughter, tears streaming down my eyes.

"Okay, I'm done," Izzie says, with a zip of her pants. "Don't you dare tell anyone anything."

"I swear I won't." I turn around to see the cup, filled halfway with yellow liquid. "Impressive, Izzie."

"Shut up," she says, turning bright red.

"Do you feel better?"

"So much better. Thank you."

"You're welcome. I'm glad to hear it," I say. Tiny hairs frame Izzie's face like a halo, and her smile is the first real one she's given me. She sure is pretty.

"Is your dad…nice?" she asks. "That seems mean to make your sister wait like that."

"My dad is the best man I've ever known. A little rough around the edges, but so am I. His only true fault was insisting my sister's bladder toughen up," I say. "I still go fishing with him every other Sunday during the summer."

"Fishing, huh? I don't think I've ever fished."

"It's more of an excuse to sit in nature and drink beer with my old man. My mom drives him crazy so he needs to get out."

"Do your parents not get along?"

"The complete opposite," I say. "My parents still smack each other on the ass when they pass each other in the kitchen. Their relationship is exactly what I want. They just believe space is healthy. So they get away from each other every now and then and swear that's the secret of success."

I pause and then say, "I thought I found that with my ex, but I didn't."

"What was her name? Your ex's?"

I smile as her face flashes in my memory. I've chosen to remember the good moments with her rather than the bad. "Hannah."

"Mine was Greg," she says. "Hannah is a pretty name."

"She was pretty." I look up at Izzie. "Not as pretty as you are, though."

More red flushes her cheeks. "Stop it."

"Am I better looking than your ex?" The way her face falls, I know the answer to that. I know what I am. I was husky as a kid. I got winded easily in PE and had a mustache in sixth grade. But I always beat kids to the punch and would make fun of myself first so we could laugh together. I became known as the funny, fat kid. Now I'm in slightly better shape and even funnier, but I'm still not winning any beauty pageants soon.

I flutter my fingers toward me. "Lay it on me. I know Henry Cavill is jealous of this jawline." I trace the line of my chin.

"Greg was...Greg was good-looking. The personality of plaster, but good-looking. He was on the soccer team in high school, and all the girls wanted him. But he chose me."

I keep my mouth shut. In high school, the girls who dated guys like that rebounded with me. It's how I got Hannah.

"Reminds me of my friend Cameron. But he was in football."

"Cameron has way more personality than Greg." Izzie shakes her head. "I can't believe I married that knucklehead."

"I'm glad I married Hannah. I loved her. I took a chance, and it just didn't work out."

Izzie sits down and crosses her legs, propping her elbows on her knees. She rests her face on her hands, staring at the concrete patterns. "I've never thought about it like that."

I sit down next to her and copy her body language. Izzie's not at all what I was expecting. Underneath the façade, she's sweet and cute and cares way more about what people think than she lets on. I wonder if her reporter persona is part of her, or if she created it. Like I created my personality so kids would laugh *with* me, not at me.

"You know, as far as bank robberies go, I'm glad I got stuck with you."

"Me too, darlin'." I raise my hand for a high five, and she smacks it.

"Oh, I'm sorry," she says her jaw drops. "I didn't wash my hands."

"It didn't happen, remember?" I say.

She smiles and jerks her head away, still embarrassed. "Right."

I can't help but smile in response.

4

IZZIE

I can't believe I peed in a corner.

In front of him.

I never peed in front of my husband, even when we had an apartment with one bathroom and he was in the shower, the water covering any sounds I could make. I would hold it for a half hour while he showered, just to push him out of the way when he came out, steam billowing behind him.

And yet, the first time I meet Thumper, I pee into a jumbo iced coffee cup, with no napkins or hand sanitizer available. It doesn't matter what he said about his sister. I am mortified.

It's hard for me not to think about it as we talk. He knows I peed in the bank vault. There's my pee, sitting on the floor, since there's no trash can. Anywhere.

There's no way Thumper will be interested in me after I pee in a cup because I can't control my bladder.

When Greg and I split, I vowed to be less shallow. Give guys a chance. Being with Greg was proof that being with a beautiful man did not mean I would be happy forever, so I reframed how I saw men. I started looking for a good person with heart and a sense of humor, rather than a striking pair of eyes.

Thumper is all of that. Talking about his sister, his dad. His parents' marriage. His way of life is fascinating. I haven't had my phone for hours, and my fingers are itching to check my email or see what's going on with my friends on Instagram. Not Thumper. He doesn't even text, and he's completely at peace being cut off from the world.

The longer we are in here, the more I'm attracted to him.

Still, he heard me pee. No man wants to date a woman he heard pee before an actual first date.

"So, why don't you have a boyfriend, Izzie?" Thumper asks.

A flush blooms on my cheeks. My voice cracks, and I cough. "I've been focusing on my career. The news never sleeps. And I don't plan to stay in Goldheart long, anyway."

"That's too bad," he says, leaning on his elbow. I'm not sure if he's genuinely disappointed. His cheeks are slack and his eyes are downturned, but that could mean a million things. "Why don't you want to stay in Goldheart?"

"It's small, and the news isn't terribly exciting here. It's a great place to live, but I want more. I want to be in a bigger market."

"Then why did you move to Goldheart in the first place?"

"Editing and having complete control over this paper...it looks good on the resume."

"I think Goldheart is very exciting."

I drop my eyes to his.

"No, seriously. A woman in a chicken costume just robbed this bank! She didn't slide a note to Ms. Keller like a coward. She came in with a shotgun. That takes balls."

"Or she's a dumbass," I say. "How much did she get? Like three grand? The charges are going to be outrageous if she's caught. False imprisonment, assault with a deadly weapon, kidnapping…"

"All of that is so sexy coming out of your mouth."

There's the heat in my cheeks again. "Are you flirting with me?"

"Maybe," Thumper says, leaning back more.

"How would I know?" I lie down as well, matching his body language, propping my elbow on the ground, resting my head on my hand. Thumper is flirting with me. Even after I peed in front of him.

"My mouth is moving," he says.

"Oh," I say. My heart drops. "How do I know you don't do this with all the other girls? How do I know I'm special?"

"You are special, Izzie St. Clair. You fascinate me."

"That makes me sound like a specimen in a lab."

"No," he says, his lips cracking into a smile. His eyes are so pretty—clear blue, and warm. I can't help matching his smile. His teeth are slightly crooked at the bottom, and his eyes crinkle at the sides.

"What fascinates you about me?" This feels like sticking my toe in alligator-infested water.

"You're smart, driven. You're divorced from your high school sweetheart, like me. We just have lots of things in common. I know it might make you want to puke, but..."

"No, it doesn't." I want to reach out and touch him. Feel his scruff against my palm, twirl my fingers in his hair. See if his lips are as soft as they look.

Thumper may be a troublemaker who's been arrested a few times, but he's not afraid to live life the way he wants to live it. He's content. That's more attractive than a perfect jawline or a clean criminal record.

He's becoming cuter to me by the minute.

"You've been asking lots of questions. Let me ask you a few," I say. I pull out my pad of paper. "It'll be for the paper, probably. Is that okay?"

"Shoot."

"Have you lived in Goldheart your whole life?"

He nods. "Born and raised."

"Is Goldheart as safe as I imagine it to be?"

Thumper nods again. "Very safe. It's why this chicken thing is surprising. Nothing like that ever happens here."

"How long have you been coming to this bank?"

"Since I was fifteen, ever since I got my very first paycheck."

I narrow my eyes. "Why did you get so much cash today?"

"That was my paycheck for this week. And I don't have a checking account, so..."

"Why don't you have a checking account?" I ask.

Thumper looks to the ground. "I don't trust banks. At all. Life was simpler when you carried your cash with you. I don't need much."

"Are you someone who has money stashed all over your house?"

The corner of Thumper's mouth turns upward. "Maybe."

"This is fascinating."

"Listen, Izzie, I'm flattered, but I highly doubt anyone will give a rat's ass about me for your paper."

"Well, maybe I want to know." I haven't written a single answer to any of these questions. It's just me, digging into what makes Thumper Thumper. How he came to be the way he is. I just want to know him better.

Investigate why I find him so fascinating. Why every time he looks at me, my heart liquifies.

Thumper's pale skin reddens, and his lips purse, stifling a smile. I smile too.

"Do you know how long we've been in here at this point?" I ask.

Thumper checks his watch. "About an hour and a half."

I notice the watch, a sleek black band with a complicated watch face. For someone who doesn't like technology, it sure looked like *lots* of technology on his wrist.

"Question: why do you have that complicated watch and a flip phone?"

"Easy. I need this for my hobbies. Compass, GPS, weather patterns. Practical. Social media—the opposite of practical."

"Makes total sense," I say with a nod. Suddenly, my stomach growls.

"Whoa there, tiger," he says, looking at my mid-section.

I've been having such a good time, I ignored the gnawing in my stomach. I substituted iced coffee for a meal again, and I'm paying for it.

"Ms. Keller probably has snacks," Thumper says, approaching her purse.

"I didn't find any in her purse," I say.

"What about the cloth bag?"

"I didn't check that."

"We should check it," he says, taking it off of the hook. We already found her phone, but eating her food seems wrong.

He must've read the concern on my face, because he says, "Ms. Keller has known me since I was a baby. She'll understand. We can always pay her back for it."

"Okay," I say as Thumper drops the bag gently on the floor, rummaging through it.

"Here you go," he says, handing me a small pocket hand sanitizer.

"Oh, thank God," I say, slathering my hands with the liquid. I've never been happier to smell like antiseptic.

Thumper continues to rifle through the bag, when suddenly he looks up. "Oh, you're going to be excited."

"What is it?"

"I don't think you're ready."

"Oh, I'm ready," I say, leaning toward Thumper. I like the proximity to him, and I want to be closer.

"For when you want to be good," Thumper says, pulling out a baggie of carrots and celery, with a small Tupperware full of a light brown substance that can only be hummus. "Or if you want to be bad." He then pulls out a small baggie of M&M's.

"I want to be good, then bad," I say, holding out my hands. Thumper hands me all of it. "I'm pretty sure this is hummus." I stick my finger in the Tupperware and taste. "Yep, it's hummus. Do you want some?"

"I can't say I've ever had hummus," he says.

"Why not? It's delicious."

"I'll take your word for it."

"Come on," I say, taking a carrot and dipping it into the hummus for him. "Try it."

"No, I'm good."

"Come on," I say, holding it out.

He looks at me the carrot and then me. "I don't know about this."

"It's so good, Thumper," I say, scooting closer. "Just try."

"Fine," Thumper says. "Hit me."

I scooch even closer, and I don't know why. Our fingers brush when he takes the carrot from me and snaps off the hummus-covered end. He nods, and chews with his mouth closed. Green flag.

When he swallows, he says, "How can you eat that shit?"

I cover my mouth and laugh. "You like sushi."

"I grew up eating fish. What the hell is hummus?"

"Ground chickpeas," I say.

"People are crazy," Thumper says. "That tastes like ass."

"I'm glad you tried it, though," I say. Our knees almost touch with our closeness, and I look at him.

I want him to kiss me, but I can't ask. It's too awkward, eating something as potent as hummus and then kissing. It can't be my idea. Thumper is used to making the first move, and I want him to.

Staring might work. I try it.

He meets my gaze. I watch his lips.

"More for me, then," I say. I don't grab a carrot or celery stick. I just stare at him.

And he does... nothing.

I'm uncomfortable, but I smile as I grab a carrot, breaking the moment.

He didn't want to kiss me.

Scratch staring as a proper flirting tactic. He must've thought I'd slather him in hummus like a baby carrot.

I can't decide if peeing in the corner or staring at him and hoping for a kiss was more mortifying. I want to die.

5

EUGENE

Does she want me to kiss her?

It seems like she does, but that could just be me reading into a situation. She *did* stare at me for entirely too long. I wipe at my face in case that gross-ass substance got on my face.

Maybe she's wondering what kind of uncultured swine I am for not liking hummus.

Izzie is a next-level woman, and this is not some Thursday at the Swift. Izzie could be feeling a certain way about me because we've bonded while stuck in a room together after a chicken pulled a gun on us.

There's no way Izzie *actually* wants me to kiss her. Or love on her. I've asked her out, and she said no. I usually give up after that. I'm not like that douchebag Tucker, who browbeats a girl until she gives in.

But I also don't want to give up on Izzie. The pull I feel toward her is stronger than anything I've felt in a long time.

Since Hannah.

I want to take Izzie in my arms and lay one on her, the type of kiss your momma warns you about. The type of kiss that makes you fall for a guy like me. Makes you get a subscription for rose-colored glasses.

Makes you forget that I have a reputation around town as a serial dater.

I'm *that* good of a kisser.

And yeah, fucking her would be nice too. But fuck is too vulgar of a word for what I want to do with her.

I've had my share of dirty encounters, but with Izzie, it would be different.

I would pull out all the romance clichés...and then pull out a few more.

Candles. Chocolate-covered strawberries. Champagne. Sweet, sweet saxophone jazz. Soft lighting. A slow and steady process of me kissing and licking every square inch of her until she's begging for an orgasm. And another one. By the time I sink my cock into her, she'll be so delirious from pleasure that she moans my name.

My real name.

The only way I will know if there's something truly going on between us is if we make it out of here. Once real life takes over and it's not just us, stuck in a bank vault.

Izzie turns away from me, staring at the corner, where the iced coffee cup full of pee resides. Her arms are crossed.

"I don't think it will be much longer." I check my watch. "It's been over two hours."

"I agree," she says. Her voice has lowered to a husky tone, sounding like she's hungover. Or emotional.

"Hey, everything will be fine," I say. I want to touch her, but I don't.

"I know," she says.

Does she want a hug? I'm not sure if I'm getting the appropriate signals. I would also love to kiss her, but I'm not sure if that is welcome.

I feel like weird Eugene in high school again, the kid who all the girls wanted to be friends with, but they didn't want to bang. I've had one too many girls talk to me to get to Cameron, women full-on sleeping with me, just to get a shot.

I know what I am. I also know what I'm not.

Izzie is the kind of woman who would be interested in a guy who has a college degree and wears suits and drinks expensive red wine and eats hummus.

Izzie raises her hand again to wipe her cheeks.

"What's wrong, Izzie?"

Her body stills. Red rims her blue eyes, tears caught in her eyelashes. She sniffles and takes a step toward me. My body goes rigid. I open my arms for a hug, but I'm secretly hoping for more.

She's leaning in.

"What are you doing?" I ask.

"I want to…"

Suddenly, the door swings open with a bang. Officer Lance Compton stands in the doorway, flanked with two cops with guns in their hands. They drop their weapons and rush in, checking the room.

I'm glad he showed up, but he had to show up *now*?

"It's about time," I say to Lance. "I thought you were never coming."

"Thumper, you have no idea the day my police force has had. We're here now."

Izzie is crying again, her shoulders shuddering with sobs.

"See? I told you everything was going to be okay."

She nods and wipes her tears. Lance sets his hands on his hips, looking between us. He points at me but looks at Izzie. "He didn't hurt you, did he?"

Izzie shakes her head violently.

"I was a perfect gentleman," I say.

"What's this?" one of the officers asks from behind me. In my horror, he's holding up Izzie's cup full of her urine.

"It's mine," I say, looking at the officers. "Izzie had a cup for me to use. We were in here for a really long time."

"Gross, Thumper," Lance says as the officer, still holding it, walks past us and out the door.

"What happened to the chicken robber?" I ask.

Lance looks down at the ground. "She caused two accidents, stopped the car, and began running through the field toward the Woody Finch Brewery. We tackled her and handcuffed her."

"Who was it?"

"Julie Hughes."

I bend over, laughing from deep in my gut. Julie and I went on a couple dates, but I skedaddled so fast when she insinuated I would be a good father to her little girl, Merrett. Her bitch of an ex ran out on them, and she was desperate to make her family whole. I got spooked and left.

I didn't know they were having money problems, but she would do anything for her child, and it made sense with the vigor she pursued me to be Merrett's new daddy. A memory suddenly pops into my head. I remember a photo from her mantle of her dressed as a chicken for her daughter's birthday party.

"Did someone pick up her daughter Merrett?" I ask.

"Julie's parents have been notified, and they already had her after school today."

I've met them; they're good people. I nod. "What about Ms. Keller?"

"She had a good scare. She has a couple bumps and bruises, but she'll be fine."

A whoosh of breath leaves my lips. Thank God.

"We got everything else taken care of. Everything will be fine," Lance says. "There's nothing you two need to worry about. We'll just take your statements and you can head home."

"Good," I say. I'm worried about Merrett, though, that little girl will be without her momma.

I just don't understand how a man can leave his child like that. If he hadn't left, she might've not needed to rob a bank.

There's a sliver of guilt that I couldn't step up for Julie, be the man she needed me to be.

Like I can't be that man for Izzie.

Any connection from being stuck together evaporated when the police busted open the door.

"That's great," Izzie says. "Would you mind giving me an interview? Or a quote?"

Izzie flips open the pad of paper I gave her, her gaze trained on Lance.

Yeah, it was all in my head, whatever this *almost* was.

So I smile as Izzie writes down facts and quotes for the paper as I smile, ready to get the hell out of here.

6

IZZIE

"Well, that's it, then," Thumper says, teetering on his boots after we gave our statements to the police and I got my interview.

It feels weird to leave Thumper now after being with him for the past three hours. It's like we're strangers again.

I don't like it. I don't like it at all.

I rip the pages I need out of his notebook and hand it to him. He waves it off.

"Keep it. Take care, Izzie," he says, leaning in and brushing his lips against my cheekbone. My eyelashes flutter close, but his feather-soft kiss is too quick on my skin.

I thought we were going to kiss back in the vault, but we didn't. Maybe I imagined our moment, and now it's gone. There were two separate instances where I thought it was possible, but looking back, I'm not so sure.

"Thank you," I say. "For everything. See you around?"

"Of course," he says, walking toward his truck. "I can't wait to read your article. Make me look good."

"Of course."

He lingers for a moment, and then he lifts his hand in goodbye and climbs into his truck.

Did he want to kiss me? He watched my lips like he was planning a strategy. We stood, staring at each other, waiting for a lightning bolt of inspiration to hit us. All I'm obsessing about is the almost moments we had, not the fact I was held at gunpoint by a single mother wearing a chicken costume.

The robbery is the furthest thing from my mind, because all I can think about is *him*.

As I drive home, all our moments cycle through my consciousness—how we joked, how we got to know each other, how I've never felt so protected and cared for in such a short time with any man. I got to know Thumper ten times better than anyone I've dated since my divorce. It crushes me he didn't follow up on his date invitation.

If he would've asked again, I would've said yes. Yes, one hundred times over.

But he didn't even get my phone number.

I spend all night thinking about that, when a normal person would be replaying the gun in their face.

It's bothering me until my friend, Addison Goodwin, comes to visit me the next morning, after my sleepless night.

Addison is my friend from high school, and we discussed her visiting me for months before we planned this weekend. She recently got married to our mutual friend, Kirk, so I wanted to give her some space. Thankfully, Kirk went to New York for the weekend to a bachelor party, so it felt like the perfect time for Addison to visit.

She gives great advice, so I can't wait to tell her about Thumper.

Addison shows up on my doorstep with two bags full of food and a bottle of wine tucked under her arm. She went vegan four years ago, so she brings her own food everywhere. There's more food than clothes hanging from her arms.

"Who has the cat?"

"Kirk's sister took Pancake for the weekend." She hands me the bottle of wine. "I'm worried one won't be enough."

Especially if we talk about what happened. I texted her last night to tell her what happened, but she doesn't know I caught feelings for my hostage partner.

It's noon, but I grab the wine bottle by the neck. "Do you want to open it now? I could use some."

"Absolutely! I'm on vacation!"

I walk into my tiny kitchen and find my corkscrew. After I pop the cork and pour us two hearty glasses of wine. I hand one to Addison. We grab our spread of veggies, hummus, and crunchy vegan snacks and walk to my loveseat, which doubles as my kitchen table. I typically don't eat vegan food, but Addison always makes everything so tasty and delicious.

The hummus makes me think of Thumper.

"Tell me everything," Addison says, taking a sip of wine. "How are you holding up after yesterday?"

"I called my therapist and booked an appointment."

"Excellent, great."

"There is one thing, though."

Addison rests her hand on my leg, already assuring and calming.

"I was stuck in there with this guy..."

"Oh," Addison says, resting her chin on her hand, eyes wide and attentive.

I go through everything. I talk about the robbery, the pee, my staring after hummus, the two almost-kiss times and how I wished he would've done it. Addison is a great impartial third party—she doesn't live here, and she's never met Thumper, so all she knows is what I'm telling her. I blabber on and on, drinking wine quickly as I talk.

"You said he has a reputation in town? Of dating around?"

I nod. "His best friend Cameron was worse than he is, but now he's madly in love with the event planner at their family's brewery. Like, they're going to get married and have babies."

"So, you're not sure if Thumper wants to settle down or not."

"I'm not sure," I say, taking another sip of wine. "I mean, I'm twenty-nine years old. I'm getting too old for a meaningless fling. I want a husband, a partner. I don't think a guy who is ready hangs out at the town bar every night."

"I thought you wanted your career now," Addison points out. I did say that, often. After my divorce, love was the last thing on my mind. But something about Thumper is breathing life into a desire I thought I wouldn't see again for a long time.

"I do, but I don't know," I say, swirling the wine in my glass. "I froze in that robbery. I cried. I lost my mind, Addison.

How am I going to handle stories where the stakes are much higher when I'm doing more high-profile reporting?"

"Getting held at gunpoint is so scary," Addison says. She pulls me into her, enveloping me in her lavender scent. Her hugs can soothe most of my ailments.

"It was, and I could barely deal with it in the moment. What if I'm kidnapped doing a story? Or tortured? Or killed? Or worse?"

Addison's eyes bulge. "Could that happen in Goldheart?"

I shake my head with a laugh. "Highly unlikely."

"Good," she says. "You mentioned this guy asked you out and you said no. Why don't you ask *him* out?"

"What? Nooooo," I say, flapping my hand in dismissal.

"Kirk and I would've been together a lot sooner if I had made the first move," Addison tells me. "We spent so much time dancing around what was going on that I still kick myself for not saying something sooner. It all worked out the way it was supposed to, obviously, but I'll never know if I would've gotten more time with him. That he was mine. I should've been braver."

"Your situation was entirely different, though," I say. "You were best friends for so long. I just spent three hours in a bank room with a guy I had only heard of through town gossip."

"Still, time is precious," Addison says. "I say ask him out. See what happens. You don't want to be too late and spend the rest of your life wondering if it could've been different. If that one decision could've changed the whole trajectory of your life."

I balance my wine glass on my bent knee, thinking how my life would go if I didn't take a shot. My year in Goldheart would be up, I'd be off to a bigger market with more dangerous stories, things a whole lot scarier than a bank robbery, and this town would be a distant memory. But I'd still think about Thumper.

It might fizzle out into nothing if we go out, but I want to try.

"So, I just go up to him and say, 'hey, I want to date you'?"

Addison nods. "Pretty much."

"I've never asked a guy out before," I say, the tingles of nerves shooting down my fingers. Every guy has pursued me. I wouldn't have said anything to Greg if he didn't say something first. I have nothing to go off of with Thumper, but I want to see if we could be something. At least I would know if I tried.

"You're nervous," Addison says, smiling.

"I'm sweating," I say, pulling my shirt away from my body.

Addison shrugs a shoulder. "How hard can it be? Ooh, practice a speech or something. Pretend like I'm him," she says, facing me, closing her eyes.

I breathe in and out. It's weird, but it's just my friend, who knows none of these people.

"Thumper, would you like to go out on a date? With me?"

"Yes," Addison says with a comically low voice. She switches back to her cheerful tone. "See? It wasn't that hard."

"You're not Thumper."

Addison takes a sip. "From everything you told me about him

and what he said to you, he sounds like a good guy. At the very least, he'll probably be flattered. He's single, right?"

"Right," I say.

Addison grows quiet, staring at my couch cushion. Usually, that means she's about to drop a truth bomb, the kind of sentence that'll haunt you for weeks. I can feel it coming.

"You need to have more confidence, Izzie," she says.

"Wow," I say. I'm not used to criticism from her.

"I mean it. You're so talented and smart. Any guy would be lucky to go out with you. If this Thumper guy is worth anything, he'll see that and won't say no. If he does, well, you'll know, and you can move on."

"You're right. I'll ask him. I have to find him, though. His phone barely works."

"What?" Addison asks. "That's strange."

I smile, thinking about our talks in the bank vault, how we laid on the cool concrete, looking at the ceiling. How he knows me better than guys I've dated for months. How he saw my soul. How he protected me.

"He's special." The trauma of the robbery was manageable because I had Thumper. He made me feel safe. He turned a stressful situation into an experience.

When we go to bed, I stare at the ceiling, thinking about Thumper.

I have to be brave.

Fearless.

For the first time in my life, I'm going to ask a man out. And

7

EUGENE

I t's been two weeks since I was held up at the bank with Izzie, and I ache, missing her.

I've stopped by the paper twice, but both times she wasn't there. Miriam, the part-time receptionist, is getting suspicious, and she's dangerous when she sniffs out gossip. I've gone to Little League games in case she's there covering a story. There was a small brush fire right outside of town and I stopped there, just in case she was at the scene.

I even got the haircut I've been putting off for six months.

I hoped fate would work its magic and I would run into her and tell her how I missed her, how those three hours in the bank vault were the best time I've had in maybe my whole life.

Then, a romance author happened.

Whitney is my buddy Cameron's girlfriend Annie's friend, a woman new in town. According to Annie, Whitney writes a book every two months, and she's become known as the laptop pianist at Gold Roast, our local coffee shop. She chops the keys of her MacBook like it owes her money.

It does in a way, I suppose.

She has this flirtation going on with Reid Finch, Cameron's brother, who is the most straight-laced motherfucker I've ever met. He used to teach history at the high school, and he reads thick books on American presidents for fun. Now he brews beer at the family brewery, Woody Finch, and his beer is damn good. Makes him tolerable once he starts using big words and talking about topics I don't give a shit about.

Supposedly Reid is playing dirty, and Whitney needs some arm candy to make him jealous.

That's where I come in. I may be in the bargain candy section, but I'm still a snack.

I'm being paraded around Woody Finch as Whitney's date to force Reid's hand. Whitney's tits are pushed to the high heavens, and they're nice, but for once in my life, I don't care about cleavage.

Of all the days to run into Izzie, she has to be here when I'm posing as the delicious morsel I am.

She's drinking beers with Tara, the owner of Gold Roast. She doesn't see me as she reacts at something Tara says, throwing back her head in laughter, her whole body full of joy.

I want to make her laugh again. I want to make her smile. I just want her.

Maybe she's not as affected as I am. Maybe she's forgotten all about me in the past two weeks.

Whitney and I sit, and she immediately fixes her bra. I ask her what beer she wants, and she orders a Night Music, which is Reid's best beer, in my opinion. It's a stout that actually does something for me, and I decide I want one as well as I head up to the counter.

Izzie sees me, and her face drops. I wave my arm wildly, but she stays frozen in her seat.

"Izzie!" I call, as I walk over to her table.

Izzie stands up, wearing a form-fitting long-sleeved shirt and tight jeans, much more my style than Whitney's intimidating leather getup. Izzie's hair is braided, and I don't let my mind travel to the thought of tugging it during the act of lovemaking.

"Making love" is a term I've always cringed at, but now I get it. As kids, my sister and I would get nauseous every time my parents mentioned making love, proclaiming it in front of us constantly. They often ask about my sex life; this family has zero boundaries and filter.

I've fucked many women in my life, but I want to *make love* with Izzie. Take my time. Explore her until she's overcome with desire and so wet I slip in like I belong there. Let her feel my signature move, the Great Thump, over and over again, until she's shaking with pleasure.

I might have to create a new move just for her.

However, I'm a gentleman. I'll wait for her, I'll take her to dinner, I'll ask her questions to find out more about that fascinating mind. Learn all of her dreams and figure out how to make them happen.

I want to take the first step by buying her a beer.

8

IZZIE

"He's here." Tara points. "Look!"

Oh, I look alright. Whitney looks ten times hotter than I ever will, with her giant breasts heaved up her chest, her shapely legs encased in leather leggings.

We knew they would be here of course, since Whitney discussed this outing with us at Annie's birthday party. She wants to make Reid, one of the Finch brothers, jealous, but I feel like I'm jealous too.

I look down at my beer. We've been nursing them for over an hour, waiting for Whitney and Thumper to show. I've never stalked a man, and it's clear I suck at it.

However, the minute he walked in, I felt a mix of nervousness and elation.

When he walks to the bar, he sees me, and I stand up.

"Hey, Izzie," he says with a huge grin as he approaches me.

Act casual. Act less stalker-y.

"Hey, Thumper," I say, shoving my hands in the back pockets of my jeans. "So, Whitney, huh?"

"Not really," he says. "I'm doing a favor. Let's just say I'm being used."

I turn to see Reid, hovering over Whitney. The way he's looking at her, I'm surprised they're not making out on top of the table.

Thumper looks at me like a friend. A good friend.

Whatever. *Be brave, Izzie.*

"I heard something about that. I'm glad you're not *with*-with her," I say.

"Not when you're around," he says. He turns to the bar and motions me along with him. "Do you want a beer? My treat."

"Sure," I say, looking up at the board. "I've been drinking Gold Dust. What else is good?"

"Prospector IPA is good, according to Cameron," he says. Shiloh is working the counter, and Emily Finch has joined her to help out with the line. I have approximately thirty seconds to say what I'm going to say.

"Listen," we say at the same time. I giggle, and he laughs too.

"You first," Thumper says.

"Listen, Thumper, I had a great time in the vault with you, considering everything, and I was wondering…"

"Next!" Emily asks. "Thumper, you're up."

"Sir, you can go ahead of me," Thumper says to the older gentleman behind me, who moves forward to Emily.

I heave a breath and look at the ground. "I was wondering if you would go out with me. Like on a date."

My stomach drops and my palms instantly sweat, but his face brightens.

"Of course," he says. "However, I would like to pick you up, and I will pay. I want to plan the date too."

"No, no, I asked you…"

He shakes his head. "That's the conditions of my acceptance of your proposal."

"Does Friday work for you? Six o'clock?"

"Yes, it does," he says. "I look forward to it."

"Good," I say, smiling. I grab a tiny golf pencil the Finches use for their flight selections and write my address and phone number on the back of a slip of paper in shaky hand-writing.

"I'll see you Friday at six o'clock," I say, hunching my shoulders with a huge grin as I walk back to Tara.

"So, what did he say?" Tara asks.

I try not to squeal. "We're going out Friday!"

"Damn, maybe I should start asking men out."

"What about Owen?" I ask. Owen is Goldheart's resident vet and comes into Gold Roast daily. They've struck up an easy friendship, but Tara is worried she's gotten friend-zoned.

"Shut up," she says. "We're focusing on your happily ever after right now."

I look at Thumper, and he waves to me as he talks to Emily.

"Let's hope so."

Eugene

WELL, color me surprised. I've never been asked out, ever. Actually, that's a lie—one of Cameron's asshole football teammates had his fuck buddy ask me to Homecoming as a joke. My ego soared high, just to crash into the asphalt.

This is not a joke. The absolute goddess, Izzie St. Clair, asked me, Eugene "Thumper" Walker, out. On a date.

I grin like a damn fool as I approach Emily Finch, who smirks just like the rest of her family. Like they know all the good gossip around town, just because they serve alcohol.

"You look happy," Emily says.

"Sometimes good things happen to good people."

"I hope that's the truth. What can I get you, Thump?"

"Two Night Musics and one Prospector IPA."

"Coming right up."

I point to Reid, who has left Whitney at our table and is walking to the back like she just made fifteen sexual innuendos in a row. "Does your brother want to get with Whitney?"

"Reid?" she asks, jutting her bottom lip out in thought as she pulls a Night Music, its dark color filling a pint glass.

"Do you think he can handle a woman like her?"

"I don't know," Emily says. She sets two pints down, and the IPA in a snifter glass. "Who is the IPA for?"

I smile. "Izzie St. Clair."

Emily looks me up and down. "I heard about the bank vault. Are you and Izzie okay?"

I look at her, her gaze hitting mine, her smile returning to her lips. "We're great. The best thing that ever happened to me."

"Is there something going on with you two?" Emily asks.

"I hope so." I hand Emily exact change and tuck a ten in the tip jar.

Emily winks. "Good luck. Don't break her heart."

"I refuse to," I say, picking up the beers. I stop by Izzie's table.

"Here you go, my lady," I say, putting it down. Tara has an inch left, and my heart sinks. Where're my manners?

"I'm sorry, Tara, did you need another beverage? I can get one for you…"

"It's okay. I'm driving," she says.

I hover for a second, and I drop a kiss on Izzie's head. If she lets me on our date, I'm going to give her a goodnight kiss that will ruin all other goodnight kisses for her. I cannot wait to show her a good time. Whether it's a romantic as fuck date, or it's lovemaking afterward, or both.

Truth can be stranger than fiction, and it looks like my ex-hookup dressed as a chicken has orchestrated my own happily-ever-after.

9

IZZIE

"Mom, I have to go," I say, holding two dresses still on their hangers up against my body in quick succession. Which one is better? Which one would be cuter?

"I'm just asking if you've applied for those jobs yet."

"No, I haven't," I say.

"Let me know the *second* you do so I can start praying," she says. "What are you up to tonight?"

"I'm going on a date."

"A *date*?" Her voice raises two octaves. I could be a celebrated journalist and win a Peabody, but nothing screams success more to my mother like a man and a ring on your finger.

I finally say goodbye to my mom as I settle on the blue dress and pull my T-shirt off over my head. I worked from home today, so I barely left the couch with my laptop and didn't put on a bra.

I'm so nervous, I can't think straight. I'm going on a date. For the first time in months.

It's not just a dating app date, where it's fifty-fifty I'll get a dick pic immediately after. This is a good guy, who I get along with, who makes me feel safe, who might actually be a good thing.

The best thing I've found in Goldheart so far.

Three weeks ago, all I wanted was to get out of this town, move to a larger city, and hustle so hard finding the news that I could lose myself.

Now Goldheart is working its magic on me.

Even if I'm stressing over a dress for a date.

I check my phone. Five fifty-eight. I hear the rumble of an engine and look out the window to see Thumper's black truck pulling in, just in time. He gets out, wearing a pressed shirt and no hat on his head, and he's holding a bouquet of pink roses.

I've never received flowers from a man, ever. I could cry.

A gentle knock, and I open the door to Thumper looking sheepish. His smile is tentative.

"Hi," I say.

His eyes widen as he looks me over. "Wow, Izzie. You're the prettiest thing I've ever seen." I blush as he hands me the bouquet of flowers. "I tried to find a bunch that smelled like you did at the brewery, but none of them came close."

Oh my God, that's the sweetest thing. When I inhale the tangy scent of the flowers, I sneeze. Thumper's face falls.

"I'm sorry, I didn't mean…"

"It's fine." I laugh. "Come on in. I need to find a vase."

Thumper walks into my place, his boots clicking on my hardwood floor. My apartment is small, but I've done my best to make it homey. Light green couches and dark green throw blankets, a fun accent pillow with birds, a bookshelf holding my favorite books, including ones beaten and torn from my childhood. Thumper wanders around with his hands in his pockets, taking it all in.

"Your place is really nice," he says, nodding as he walks around. He runs his hand over my throw blanket, and I wish his palm was skimming my skin.

"Thanks," I say, filling a vase with water and cutting the stems down. I drop the flowers in and fluff the blooms. I set it in the middle of my breakfast bar.

"Perfect," I say. I walk around the kitchen and wrap my arms around Thumper's shoulders, pulling him in. I lay a kiss on his cheek, and he leans into my lips, his arm wrapping around my waist.

"Thank you," I say, staying in his embrace.

"I get a kiss already?" he asks.

"Of course," I say.

His cheeks turn red, and he looks down at the ground with a big smile. It's like he's not the biggest playboy in town, used to women throwing themselves at him left and right.

His heart is so much different than the Thumper the town knows.

Eugene is sweet, thoughtful. Protective.

"Let's go," he says, taking my hand, interlacing his fingers with mine. "I have a special surprise planned."

"Oh?" I ask.

"Come on," he says, pulling me to my door. I grab my purse and a light cardigan, following Thumper wherever he wants to take me.

AFTER WE SING Tim McGraw songs at the top of our lungs in his truck, he pulls into the parking lot for the lake, empty now that tourist season is over. There's a couple people enjoying some drinks on the beach, and it looks like we're about to join.

"I didn't know what you'd like, so I got a little bit of everything," Thumper says, as he gets out of truck and grabs a large cooler from the bed of his truck. He hands me a thick flannel blanket and a bag. He leads me to a spot by a pile of large rocks, partially secluded from the other beach-dwellers.

"I hope this is okay," Thumper says, opening the cooler to show stacked to-go containers. As he pulls them out and opens the lids, I'm greeted with sushi roll after sushi roll, coated with all different sauces, decorated with all sorts of fish. I look at him as the food keeps coming, at least a hundred dollars' worth of sushi.

"Thumper," I say, my mouth agape at all the food, "it's so much."

"Don't worry, it won't go to waste. If there's any left, I'll drop some off at Cameron's. That motherfucker is a bottomless pit. I don't know where he puts it."

I smile as he offers me chopsticks or a plastic fork, and I pick the chopsticks. He does too. I pick a random roll, and my eyes bulge at the flavors exploding in my mouth. I take another piece, and the spice hits me. I cough.

"That's a sneaky one. They call it the fire-alarm sauce."

"It's so good," I say. My eyes water, and I fan myself. "I swear."

"Here," Thumper says, pulling a canned beer out of his bag. It's Prospector IPA, the one he bought me the other night. "I picked up each of the Woody Finch IPAs. I'm not sure which one you liked more…"

"No, this is perfect," I say. He hands me a plastic cup. He's literally thought of everything. I've never felt more special in my whole life.

"This is so much. Thank you," I say. "I'm saying thank you a lot."

"I don't mind it," Thumper says, popping another sushi piece in his mouth. He chews like he's savoring it, letting the moment soak into his bones. He hasn't checked his phone once, done nothing but focus all of his attention on me.

This is how to live—in the moment, present with another human. I've had a few first dates, and they're a sliding scale of terrible—getting to know the person, feeling them out, determining whether they want to have sex with you or murder you or both. With Eugene, I got to know him in the direst of circumstances.

I'm falling harder with each moment.

"This is already the best first date I've ever been on."

"Yeah?" he asks. "You deserve the best. I want you to feel that and believe it."

"I do. This is perfect, Eugene, thank you," I say. "Is it okay I call you Eugene? I know not everyone does but…"

He shakes his head. "I really like the way you say it. Feel free to call me Eugene all you like."

He takes another bite, and I look at him, really look at him. If I had seen him on the street or let first impressions get the better of me, I wouldn't be here with him.

I had been so wrong.

"I will," I say, cradling his cheek in my palm. He leans into it and closes his eyes, like he's absorbing my touch with his whole body.

Thumper takes his hand and rests it on the back of my neck. His touch singes my skin as his thumb plays with the stud that adorns my earlobe. He stares at me like he's in no rush, knowing the anticipation is the best part of any first kiss.

When he pulls me to him, I taste the spice on his lips, the coolness of the beer in his mouth. My body heats as we kiss, turning our heads from side-to-side, taking our time. Letting this moment exist as it is. Without a past or a future.

His mouth moves and mine does too, our tongues drifting into each other's mouths without a care in the world. This kiss feels like sinking into a hot spring after a cold day. It fits so perfectly into the rhythm of our date. When we pull away, we're breathless. Our foreheads touch, and I swallow, the sips of breath still ramped up.

"Wow," is all he can say, and I feel the same.

"This is the most perfect day," I say as I rest my hands on his shoulders, the soft material of his flannel. "The flowers, the sushi, you."

"Darlin', I could get rid of the rest of this, and your sweet lips would be enough to get me through most anything."

That is the cheesiest thing a man has said to me. And I loved every word of it.

I sit back, trying to have some semblance of a date instead of immediately jumping on him and asking him to have me right here on this beach. "So, is this the best part of town? The lake?"

"It's pretty great. It's even better when the tourists leave."

"You don't realize how empty a town is until they leave," I say. "The sidewalks were so crowded all summer. There were people everywhere."

Eugene nods. "They keep our town afloat, that's for sure. I'm helping on new builds of second homes going in around the lake"—he points to the opposite shore—"and it's growing, even if it doesn't seem like it."

"I don't want Goldheart to grow," I say. "I'm starting to see why you like it."

Eugene chuckles. I notice his lips are pink and swollen from our kiss earlier. "I don't want it to grow either, but I care about the people in the town. We need the tourists and the newcomers." He grins at me. "I know I need a certain newcomer."

He grabs my side, catching the most ticklish part, right under my ribs. I squirm away, giving away my vulnerability.

"Ah," he says, tapping his temple. "I'll remember that for later."

"Don't use it for evil."

"I never use stuff like that for evil, darlin'. Only for fun."

I boop him on the nose with the clean side of my chopstick, as his cheeks rise in a full-out grin. I pick up a new roll piece, and it's even better than the first. Is that pesto on top?

"Oh my God," I say, covering my mouth.

Eugene's lips break into a wide grin. His teeth are slightly crooked, but it adds to the charm of his smile.

"Once we're done eating, I want to take you to a spot. It's a local thing. Only Goldheart townies know about it. And since you've been involved in the first bank robbery in Goldheart in three years, you're officially a townie."

His thumb grazes my cheek and I sigh.

"That sounds fun."

"Go ahead and eat until you're about to burst," Thumper says, pointing at all the sushi. "I don't want to give anymore to Cameron than I have to."

I SNEAK one more kiss before we pack up the cooler and finish off our beers. The beer makes my brain hazy. We walk back to the truck, and he offers his hand so I can step up into the cab. His thumb rubs the back of my hand and my heart flutters.

We drive a couple miles to another parking lot of the local used bookstore and coffee stand on the side of the road. Once we get out, Thumper grabs my hand and points to an opening in the brush, a tree line cresting over the buildings.

I point to my flats made of cloth, shoes not meant to walk on uneven ground. "I don't think I wore the right shoes."

"It's fine. I'll carry you if your feet start to hurt," he says, pulling me into the forest. It drops ten degrees, and I shiver, my bare arms covered in goosebumps. I don't know where we're going, and if I didn't feel so safe with Eugene, I would be worried.

"Are you cold, darlin'?" Eugene asks, stretching his arm out. "Come snuggle with me."

"Okay," I say. The palm of his hand is calloused and rough, but it's comforting on my arm as I wrap it around my midsection. Electricity courses through our embrace as we walk further into the woods. I see pockets of sky as we walk down a path that's only wide enough for a single file. When we reach our destination, I gasp.

In the middle of a clearing is a structure made of stone, a wishing well. It's straight out of my fairy tale dreams, something I would speak into as a little girl, hoping my wish would come true. A few months ago, I would've been wishing for a more exciting journalism opportunity, far, far from here.

Going through the robbery, being with Eugene, has confused me to my core, making me rethink everything. I love my Goldheart apartment. I love my coffee shop. I love how there's not a single chain restaurant in city limits, that everything is owned by a Goldheart resident, that you're doing business with the heart of the town. How this town was founded by dreamers, brave men and women who wanted to make a better life for themselves and their families.

How everyone says hello, no matter how well they know you.

Yes, the town has been slow to warm to me, but that didn't stop them from being kind.

This wishing well solidifies what I know about this town. Sometimes everything you're looking for is right here.

"What is the story with this?" I ask, approaching it. Moss snakes through the grout between the stones, and there's a musty smell creeping up from the depths of the well. The wood of the basket looks worn and crumbly, not sturdy at all.

"I don't know when it was built," Eugene says, standing close to me, resting his hand on my lower back. "It's been here since before I was born. My sister loved it so much when we were kids. She always acted like a princess making a wish."

He leans in and whispers, "It's your turn. What will you wish for?"

I look at him and close my eyes, letting the breeze play with the tiny hairs around my face. I place my palms on the lip of the well, asking for clarity. *Please tell me where I'm supposed to go. What I'm supposed to do.*

If I'm meant to stay here. If I'm meant to be with Eugene.

Also, I would love one really good orgasm.

"Are you done, darlin'?" he asks.

"I am," I say, leaning into his embrace. "Thank you for bringing me here."

I lean in for another kiss. His lips entrance me, making my body warm amidst the coolness of the trees and forest. His arms wrap around my back, and I feel so cared for, so cherished. He kisses me like it's been something he's been hoping for. Wishing for.

When we pull apart, we're breathless.

"Do you want to come back to my place?"

"I thought you would never ask," he says. "I can't wait to make you feel good, if you want me to."

I swallow. "I do."

"Good," Eugene says, nuzzling my neck.

10

EUGENE

I call my neighbor, Mrs. Epstein, and she agrees to let my dog, Bambi, hang out with her for the night, just in case. I'm sure my dog will be treat-drunk when I get back tomorrow morning, but I don't care.

I drive my truck like the Goldheart cops are chasing me.

I pull out with a squeal from the parking lot, doing ten over the speed limit, passing cars moving too slow on our country roads.

I want Izzie naked now.

When we pull into her apartment complex, I search her face, body language for any hesitation. She just gives me those big blue eyes, and I think she's ready to be made sweet, sweet love to. It would be my absolute pleasure to make this a night never to forget.

"Wait there," I say as I walk around the truck, opening her door and offering her my hand.

"Why, thank you, good sir," she says, grabbing my hand and stepping down into the gravel. I circle my arm around her shoulders, walking her to her door. My arms wrap around her waist as she fiddles with her key, unlocking her apartment.

This place smells like her, rich and warm, intriguing and beautiful.

"We're here again," she says.

"We are," I say, kicking off my boots. She kicks off her flats and clasps her hands behind her back, swinging back and forth so her skirt can flutter.

I don't say a word before I grab her and kiss her. It escalates from sweet to hot in seconds, me lifting her by her bottom so her long legs wrap around me. I push her hair away from her face as I press her against her wall, right next to her bookshelves. Our tongues dive toward each other's, the fire building between us, like pouring kerosene on a campfire. Her lips are soft and intoxicating, I cannot get enough.

The strap of her dress is so thin, and I pull it off of her creamy shoulder as I kiss down it, getting a little moan out of her. The flesh below her collarbone is calling to me so I press my lips to it, flirting closer and closer to Izzie's breast still covered by this beautiful dress.

"May I?" I ask.

"Yes," she says as I peel the dress from her breast. She's wearing no bra, and I'm greeted with a pale pink nipple, pebbled, ready for my mouth. I swirl my tongue over it, a whoosh of air leaving Izzie's lips. I put her down, crouching in front of her body, letting my hand trail up her skirt, and feel her panties already damp from her pleasure.

Damp because of *me*.

"I'm glad I can make you feel good," I say, squeezing her

exposed breast gently as my other hand tucks itself into her underwear, feeling the silky hair that protects the most delicate part of her.

"I'm sorry I didn't have time to shave," she says.

"I prefer women like this. Natural."

I pull her underwear down, and she steps out of it, flinging it to the side. They have little flowers on it, just like this dress I'm taking off of her soon.

She arches against her wall as I push her skirt up, seeing her hips, all of her mile-long legs and the area between her thighs, the dark hair slick with her arousal for me. Pulling one of her legs onto my shoulder, I dive into her pussy, licking her from back to front, settling on her clit, suckling it, driving her mad.

"Oh my God," she says as I continue to take my time. This is not a race, and I know I can get her there. So I stay here, my tongue working her as her clit swells, as her hands land on my head.

"I'm going to come," she gasps. She shrieks a few times before coming completely undone. Her pussy spasms against my face, coating my lips with her juices, making it so I can't forget how her pussy tastes. Ever. I love it.

She pulls me up by the ears, and I kiss her, letting her taste her orgasm. She has no fear, dipping her tongue into my mouth.

"Where's your bedroom?" I ask. My cock is painfully hard in my jeans and it wants out, but I want her soft hands to be the one to free it. She nods and pulls me by the hand to the bedroom. Her bed is a queen, big enough for the both of us, decorated with a mint comforter and lacy white throw pillows.

"I need to get this off of you," I say, reaching for the back of her dress for the zipper. Izzie turns, and I see the moles on her back, decorating her pale skin. I unzip her and let the dress fall to the ground. She's naked now, and I cup her breasts from behind, then drift down to her pussy again.

"I have condoms," she says, walking to her side table. She pulls one out to hand to me, and I pin it between my fingers as I take her lips again. There's something exhilarating that a woman has protection, ready for anything, no matter what.

She pulls my shirt over my head, unbuckles my pants. When she removes my boxer briefs, my cock springs free, hard and long. I don't expect her to take me in her mouth, but she does and my head rolls back in ecstasy.

Izzie's making all the right moves, cupping my balls like they're precious, her head moving back and forth like a piston. The sight of her blond head at my cock, her naked body sprawled across her bed, with her feet kicking drives me to the brink, a place I don't want to be if I'm not inside of her.

I touch her cheeks softly as I pull her mouth off of me, using every ounce of willpower I have. I rip the foil packet and roll the condom onto my stiff-as-a-board cock, and Izzie rolls onto her back, naked and beautiful, her legs open and ready for me.

"Come and get me," she says.

"It would be my pleasure," I say, crawling toward her, settling between her legs, taking her lips with mine. Guiding myself into her, we sigh in relief as we're together, one. The first roll of my hips is delicious, as I feel how warm she is, how open she is, how connected we are, how we just *fit*. I want this feeling to last forever. I've never felt like this with any other woman before.

I take her hand and lace my fingers with hers as I thrust into her, making it slow and deliberate. I do it again, and her nails claw into my ass like she's enjoying every single inch of me.

"How are you feeling, darlin'?" I ask, rolling into her, the pleasure coursing through my body. Her eyes are closed in ecstasy as she exhales, letting out a delicious moan.

"Wonderful," she says, as another sound exhales. Her fingers dig into me, motioning me to quicken my pace. I thrust into her harder, faster, and her sounds give me the feedback I need. We come undone, and I arch my neck, letting the surge rip through me. Her pussy pulses at the same time as I empty into the condom, filling it to the brim. My whole body feels the electricity of the moment, and when it's done, I just hug her.

"That was...amazing," she says, reaching up to kiss me. I take her lips, punctuating this moment, knowing it won't be the last time tonight we do what we just did.

I anchor myself as I pull out and fall in next to her, draping my arm over her stomach. I kiss her forehead, her cheek, her nose. She looks blissed out.

She stretches her arm over her head, her eyes still closed.

"Perfection," she says.

Looking at her, I can't help but think the same.

There's a clang in my kitchen, and it makes me sit up straight.

The memories of last night flood back into my consciousness, and I flop back down into my sheets. Sheets that were christened last night. Three times.

Turning my head, my eyes bug. Eight-thirty. I never sleep in this late, ever.

We spent all night exploring each other's bodies and drifted off to sleep around two. Before I fell asleep, I told Eugene I needed to be somewhere at ten, an arts festival on Main Street. I set my alarm for nine, just in case.

The smell of breakfast drifts under my nostrils, and I hear another clang in my kitchen. If he's making me breakfast, he's forgiven.

"Shit," I hear, and I chuckle. I get out from under my covers and grab a T-shirt from my chair, pulling it over my naked body. I walk out to see Eugene in his white undershirt, his back facing me. When he turns around, he smiles.

"Hey, darlin', sorry to wake you up," he says, a spatula in hand. "I know you have to be in town at ten so I scrounged up some breakfast. I hope you like eggs and bacon."

"I love it," I say, as I walk to him, falling into his arms. The bacon sits in a pool of grease, and the eggs are perfect over medium. There's piles of toast, perfectly golden brown. He's pulled out my jam and butter, a knife balanced on the containers.

"Here you go," Eugene says, handing me a plate with the offerings. I take it to my breakfast bar, climbing onto the chair, my bare ass on the seat. I will have to clean it later, but I'm distracted by the man cooking me breakfast, being all-around adorable.

While I butter my toast, he sets some coffee down in front of me.

"Thank you," I say, taking a sip. He made it just how I like it.

He sips his own and plates two eggs with some strips of bacon, sitting down next to me.

"I could get used to this," he says, pushing my hair out of my face. He kisses my neck as I chew, biting off the crispy bacon, the salty grease delicious on my tongue.

"Me too," I say, kissing him once I swallow my bite.

"I wish I could hang out with you today, darlin'," Eugene says. "Make this the longest date I've ever been on."

"I wish I could too."

He massages my neck, his thumb working my tight muscles. He gives massages too? He's literally perfect.

"What are you doing tonight?" he asks.

"Shoot, I have a friend thing. Tara and I have standing Saturday night wine dates." I never believed in canceling plans with friends to hang out with a guy, so I need to go, just on principle. I missed one Saturday because of Addison, and I need to gab with Tara. I want time to talk about him, moon about him, revel in delicious anticipation.

But I know that I—and my pussy— will miss him. "How about tomorrow?"

"I can't tomorrow," Eugene says. "I have some handyman things I need to take care of, and Bambi and I need to spend some quality time together."

My eyes bulge. Who's Bambi?

"Bambi is my dog," Eugene says with a laugh. "You should've seen your face."

"You have a dog? What's she doing right now?" I don't know how Eugene could melt my heart more, but hearing he has a dog named Bambi does it. Still, I'm worried about the dog. Was she left alone all night long?

"Don't worry, I got a babysitter," Eugene says, pulling out his wallet. He pulls out a small photo of a black lab puppy, the cutest thing I've ever seen. That he carries an actual photo in his wallet of his dog, rather than on his phone, is endearing and adorable and...hot. "Mrs. Epstein, my neighbor, loves Bambi. Gives her treats, lets her sleep on the bed. Bambi might not want to come home."

"That's so cute." I've seen Mrs. Epstein around town, and at the library. Super sweet lady. Gives great hugs.

"How about Monday night?" he asks. "I'll cook for you. You can meet my dog."

"Is that too soon? That feels like a big deal."

Eugene looks at me, his face serious. "I want to be yours, if you'll have me."

"Like boyfriend-girlfriend?"

"Yeah," he says, his gaze pleading. "What do you say?"

Wow, it's that easy?

"Sure," I say. A huge grin breaks through on my face. "Yes."

He pulls me in for a kiss, and I could burst out of my skin. I've never been asked to be a girlfriend before. When my ex and I got together in high school, it was assumed from our first date. To this day, I don't know if there were other girls at the beginning of our courtship.

I know exactly where I stand with Eugene. And it's amazing.

"What about other girls? Won't you miss them?"

"Nope," he says, shaking his head. "It might be soon to say, but you might be the one. My only one."

We kiss, and I can't help but fall under.

I never want him to leave. It will be an eternity until Monday, but I know exactly where I stand. He wants me to be his only one. It feels so easy, so natural for us to be together, that I doubt every relationship I've ever had before this.

It might be too soon to tell, but I feel like this could be forever too.

"You and Thumper? It makes sense," Tara says, pouring some more wine into my empty glass. I nod, smiling.

"Yep. He's officially my boyfriend," I say. "We talked about it this morning, and we're exclusive."

"Wow," Tara says, pouring herself some wine as well. "I did not see that coming so fast. I guess armed robbery bonds people."

"I guess so." We're sitting on Tara's deck, enjoying the breeze and the sunset. As dark enveloped her porch, she suggested we go down to her fire pit, and I'm enjoying the peace of being present, watching the flames lick the night sky.

I didn't check my phone all day, leaving it in my messenger bag as I took photos and talked to artists and creators at the art fair. Although knowing Thumper doesn't text meant I didn't need to check my phone, it felt freeing to be not tethered to my phone for adoration or dopamine hits, since I had a night of pleasure and sweetness that trumps everything. I'm riding a high so transcendent that nothing my phone can give me can compare.

"This is so great. Just being present," I say.

Tara smirks. "You haven't been on your phone as much. Is this because of Thumper?"

I nod. "It's so nice dating someone who doesn't believe in technology."

"You are totally falling in love," Tara says.

"I might be," I say. My cheeks warm at the thought.

Tara pauses and says, "I kinda knew Thumper had it in him. More than Cameron, anyway. But let's not talk about Cameron."

Tara takes a huge swig of wine. Tara slept with Cameron before he started dating our friend Annie. Cameron told Tara he didn't want a relationship with her, and it's made her skittish. I wonder if that's why she hasn't tried anything with Owen, even though they have an intense flirtation going.

"Yes, let's not," I say.

Tara balances her wine glass on her thigh. "I think Thumper is ready to settle down. Try it on for size. I always knew deep down he would be a good boyfriend."

"Well, I'm less than twenty-four hours in, but I can confirm."

"I bet he's a 'sweet voicemail' guy."

"Maybe," I say. "He barely uses his phone. I should check it, though, in case the paper's called me."

I pull out my phone and see two notifications for voicemails. I shimmy my shoulders in excitement and stick out my tongue.

"There is one from him," I say, opening my voicemail. One of them is Eugene, and the other is an out-of-area area code. Must be a telemarketer.

I listen to Eugene's first.

"Hey darlin', I know we just talked, but I'm leaving you a voicemail while you're at Tara's. Wanted to let you know I'm thinking about you. I can't wait to see you. Just wanted to tell you you're beautiful. Okay, bye."

I sighed as I pulled my phone away from my ear.

"Was that Thumper being sweet?"

I nod with a grin. I click to the next voicemail. My eyes bulge when I hear who it is.

"This message is for Isabella St. Clair. Isabella, this is Janine

Paulson from the *Seattle Tribune*. I wanted to talk to you about a position..."

"What?" Tara asks. I pull the phone away and swallow, my throat so tight, it hurts.

12

EUGENE

"Now, Bambi, I want you to know you're my best girl," I say to my dog as I turn the steak over on the grill in my backyard. All I hear is the thumping of a tail.

Bambi's head tilts, and I see the stream of drool leaving her mouth, looking at the dead cow I'm cooking. She's sitting pretty, but she doesn't care what I'm saying because I'm a big, dumb pushover when it comes to her brown eyes. She knows she'll get a little treat.

I got Bambi when she was a puppy, and she is the light of my life. However, she might have to sleep in her crate tonight, so I'm preparing her. I haven't brought a woman home since Cameron stopped being my wingman at the Swift, so Bambi's gotten used to being the little spoon on my bed, sprawling out on her back like she's roadkill.

I told Izzie to pack an overnight bag.

"I want you to be a little lady, Bambi," I say, pointing a spatula at her. More drool falls from her jowls. "Be polite and don't immediately smell her crotch. That's your papa's space. Got it?"

More adorable head tilts.

I reach out to scratch behind her ears, and she leans into my touch, licking my palm, telling me she will be on her best behavior. "That's a good girl," I say.

There's a knock at my front door, and I walk around to the side of the house, Bambi guarding the steaks. She's two years old, but she's a shit protection dog. She can protect me from squirrels and the occasional cat, but every person who knocks is a friend she hasn't met yet.

I open the gate and call Izzie over. She looks casual in a pair of baggy jeans and a crop top, her toned stomach peeking out. Her hair is down, and I can't help but tug it gently as I kiss her.

"I missed you so much," I say, pulling her in. Izzie smiles sadly, and my eyebrows crease. I brush her hair over her shoulders. "What's going on? Something wrong?"

She shakes her head. "Nothing. It's fine. I missed you too."

"Good," I say, kissing her again, pulling her in.

Bambi turns her head and walks toward us, her tail wagging like a hummingbird's wings, her head down as she approaches us.

"This is Bambi," I say.

Izzie crouches down, letting Bambi bathe her face with kisses. I always said that I don't trust people who don't like dogs, but I trust a dog who doesn't like a person. I got that from somewhere, but I've never heard something truer.

Bambi immediately loving on Izzie makes my heart swell. That was the last test. This gives me full permission to fall in love with Izzie.

"Okay, give the tongue a break, Bambi," I say, patting my dog on the head.

"No, I love this," Izzie says. "My family dog died two years ago, so it's been a while since I've gotten puppy kisses."

"This isn't the last time you'll get them, trust me. With what we're eating, she'll lick you for five minutes if you'll let her."

Izzie approaches the grill, her eyes large. "Those look amazing."

"Thank you. Cooking a steak is one of my five talents. How do you take yours?"

"Medium rare."

She's becoming more and more of the perfect woman. I say nothing, just kiss her. Her lips are soft, but they don't respond. My eyebrows knit together as I pull back.

"Something is definitely up. Tell me," I say.

She breathes out and looks up, her eyes huge and so blue.

"I got a call over the weekend," she says. "From the *Seattle Tribune*."

"Oh," I say, acting nonchalant, but I know what is coming. She will shake up my world, and the fantasies I've had for the last couple days may never happen. From the beginning, she's told me her career comes first. She's never wanted to stay in Goldheart.

Goldheart's not the place to be for news, I get that. And I

can't keep her from her dreams. That would be wrong of me, no matter how strong my feelings are.

Izzie nods. "They made me an offer. I had an interview six months ago, before I got the job offer in Goldheart. I became friends with a section editor on social media, but I didn't think anything of it. I thought it would never happen…"

She walks away from me to pace, and I let her. Her hands rake through her hair. She likes me, sure. But if it's between her career and a blossoming new relationship with me, she should go with the career.

Everything feels like a good sign with her, but no one knows what the future looks like. How one simple phone call can change your life.

"Have they sent the official offer?"

She nods and hands me her phone. It takes me a minute to read through the text of the email. The salary is definitely higher than the *Goldheart Gazette* could ever offer. There's only so many ads a small bakery or insurance agency can pay here. I've never been to Seattle, but that salary might not go far. I could make it work in Goldheart, but Seattle? I'm not sure.

I can't say that, though. I can't sway Izzie or tell her my opinion. She's a smart woman. She knows what's best.

"What are you going to do?" I ask, handing her phone back to her.

"I don't know," She stands there, biting her lip. The steaks are sizzling a little too much so I take them off to do something in the silence. Bambi sniffs the steaks, and I wave her away, putting her in a down. My heart feels the break that's coming, that I just found a woman who could be it for me, and she's leaving.

"I think you should take it," I say. Staring at the ground is the only way I can get through this, telling her what I think is best for her life, not what is in my heart. "You said it yourself. You wanted to get out of this town. Find a bigger market."

"I did say that," she says. She crosses her arms and stares at the same spot of concrete in my backyard that I am.

"I don't want to be the guy that keeps you from your dreams. It sounds like a great opportunity, one you've been wanting. Don't worry about me. Please don't."

"But I feel things. For you." She takes a step toward me, circling her arms around my waist. "You're the biggest surprise of my life."

"Same, darlin'," I say, kissing her neck. "Let's enjoy tonight. Pretend like everything else isn't going on."

"That sounds great," she says, kissing me quickly and snuggling into me. I hold her tightly. Bambi squeezes her body between our legs, and it makes me laugh.

"You want some love too, honey?" I scratch behind her ears, and Bambi groans, making Izzie giggle. I smile, although my heart is splitting in two. God is so cruel to me, to show me someone as beautiful, witty, and talented as Izzie, just to pull her away to Seattle.

I know in my heart this would end. I'm a lifer here in Goldheart. It's woven itself into my soul and my life, and I could never leave. This town has been my home my whole life. Life doesn't get much better than Goldheart.

As she cuts into the steak I prepared for her, and asks if it's okay to give Bambi a little bit, I decide to enjoy this moment.

For however long I have with her, I will savor it.

Izzie is special, a woman I will think about forever. However, I believe in His grace, and if He wants us to be together, well, it's gonna happen.

Until I know the answer, I'm gonna enjoy what I have, and that's the present. It's this beautiful woman eating at my table. It's my dog getting ear scratches from someone else so I can take a break. It's this wonderful meal. It's the way the breeze has a hint of hay in it, signaling fall is near.

The future can't take away this memory from me. Whether I have Izzie in my life for a week or a lifetime, it's enough simply to know her.

13

IZZIE

The next day, I hold it together until I get inside my car. Crumpling over my steering wheel, I sob so hard, I lose track of time. My phone buzzes.

An alert. *Goldheart City Council meeting, 9 a.m.*

Nothing like a boring meeting to distract me from the range of emotions I've felt since leaving Eugene's arms.

After the steaks, he crated Bambi and led me by hand to his bedroom, undressing me slowly, kissing me everywhere—my collarbone, my hip, my lips, in between my legs. When he lined up his cock and eased into me, I saw stars.

This would not last forever, but Eugene refused to talk about it.

So, we had one perfect night, free of discussions of what will happen to us, now that Seattle has presented me with an impossible situation. Get the dream I've always wanted, or stay for the possibility of a dream I couldn't have even imagined a month ago.

My thoughts distract me as I walk into the board meeting,

straightening my jacket. Since I knew I would have to go straight there from Eugene's house, I packed my work clothes, a blazer and a pair of nice jeans with a billowy blouse, so I felt professional, even if my heart twisted on the inside. A woman appears in front of me, and I'm knocked out of my daze enough to smile.

"Hello," I say.

She looks at me oddly, and I press my lips together in a polite smile.

"You're Izzie St. Clair, right?"

"That's me," I hold out my hand. "And you are...?"

"Naomi Walker," she says. "Thumper's mom."

My smile falls. The way Eugene talks about his mom is any parent's dream. He worships her, and that's when I knew he was a good one.

I'm not sure if he's mentioned me to her, but I assume so by the way she's looking at me.

"It's so nice to meet you," I say.

"No, the pleasure is all mine," Naomi says. "You know, Thumper talks about you all the time. He wouldn't stop yammering at our last family dinner."

"Oh?" I ask. My cheeks warm.

"You are very special. It's been a long time since he's told us about a woman he's seeing."

Naomi smiles, and I see the same kindness in her eyes that I see in Eugene's. How their cheeks lift with their smiles, like their whole face might crack. Her hair is highlighted and a bright pink lipstick coats her lips, but I see Thumper in her. And that makes my heart break even further.

"It was so nice to meet you," I say again. Since I don't know what will happen with Seattle, I say, "I hope we can see each other soon."

"Absolutely," she says. She pauses before she says, "I love my son, so I'm biased, but you won't meet a kinder man. He's a good one, I promise. The kind of guy women write country songs about. Not the jerks who they have to burn the house down for, but you know, the good ones. Like that song."

"The Good Ones" by Gabby Barrett. I actually listened to it on the way to the meeting and sobbed.

A month ago, I didn't think a man like that existed for me. After my divorce and the string of bad dates from apps, I focused more on my career and left love on the back burner. Maybe the one for me wasn't all the places I looked before. Maybe the right one hated technology and didn't trust banks, and the only way I would meet them is during a chicken-themed robbery. How could I have ever predicted that?

Still, Seattle was the dream. It would be wondrous for my career, seeing new things, experiencing new people. There's actually news going on there. More money, more opportunity. Not this quiet town where the only thing happening is the city council meeting and the rare bank robbery that ended well.

I'm still standing in front of Eugene's mom, and I take her hands. "You raised a good one."

"I know," she says. "I don't know if this is appropriate to say, but the fact my son picked you means you're a good one as well."

I smile sadly. "Thank you for that."

"You're welcome," she says. She puts her glasses on. "Let's get this meeting over with. These are so boring, I can't believe you cover them."

"My predecessor did too, so I just do what he did."

"There has to be more exciting things going on here," she says. "I know we don't have the crime and drama of the big cities, but there's plenty of material. This town is full of good, interesting people."

"I agree," I say, and my insides twist. How does she know that I've said this town is boring? That I've wished for a more exciting market?

"I know you knew that. After all, you were in a robbery where the assailant wore a chicken costume. I mean, if that doesn't give you hope for the potential of this town, I don't know what will." Her mouth stretches in horror as I laugh. "I'm sorry if that was insensitive."

"No, that was perfect," I say. "An absolutely perfect way of saying that."

14

EUGENE

"Please call me the minute you land," I say. I parked my truck and decided to walk in with Izzie. I waited while she got her boarding pass and checked her luggage, accompanied her up the escalator to the tram. I even went on the tram with travelers, holding their luggage or fiddling with their earphones. When it emptied and everyone scurried to the TSA line, Izzie hung back with me.

"I will," she says, crushing me in a hug. I touch her hair, trying to commit this moment to memory. When she pulls back, I notice some moisture on her cheeks. I push back her hair and kiss the tears away.

Izzie is heading to Seattle to look for an apartment and attend orientation for the job. She's waiting to submit her resignation to the *Gazette*, just in case the visit doesn't go well.

My heart already hurts. My needy dog is alarmed by the extra snuggles I've required since Izzie told me she booked her ticket. I can't stop hugging her as the TSA line piles and piles and travelers flow over us like water.

I kiss her. And kiss her again. "I'll be here when you get back."

"I know you will be," she says, pressing her lips to mine one last time before she disappears into the sea of people. She looks back and blows me a kiss.

I'm not even sure how long I stand there for. I watch her pass security and stand under the screens showing the status of flights. She watches me, and I watch her. I hold my hand up to signal goodbye, and she does the same. I walk to the outgoing tram with my head hanging down.

I fold the bill of my ballcap and pull it back onto my head, leaning against the wall of the tram as it starts moving. I have an hour and a half of driving before I get home. It will be time to think, but I know I will be thinking about Izzie the entire time.

I might let a tear or two slip out.

Why does it feel so wrong when I know in my heart it's the right thing for her?

Izzie

I'm in a group of fifteen people new to the paper, and we all eye each other like competition. Once in a while, I catch someone looking at me, and I wonder if I have a spot on my face or a stain on my blazer.

But no, they're just sizing me up.

A section editor is presenting a PowerPoint, clicking through it with the apathy of a high school student presenting a history project.

"The expectation is that you will keep your cell phone on at all times to answer our calls," the section editor says. "The news never sleeps, and if there's a breaking report, you should be eager to seize any and every opportunity."

I slouch in my seat. Goldheart had a similar policy, but it rarely happened. Once in a while, there would be breaking news and I would rush to a scene of an accident or fire, but it happened once or twice a month. Maybe it's the same with Seattle.

The section editor takes her glasses off, a sign she's about to get real.

"My first month at the *Tribune*, I was called twenty times to go out to the scene for a breaking story. I slept with my phone on full blast. Woke up my husband. I didn't care because the news is more important than anything else. We have a duty to the residents of Seattle..."

I think of Thumper. How he uses a phone that barely works and ignores it for long periods of time. I remember how nice it was to leave my phone in one place for long stretches of time on our dates.

Being chained to my phone rubs me the wrong way now.

"You will live, eat, and breathe this paper your first year. You have to pay your dues. Get ready to work harder than you've ever worked. We've picked you out of thousands of applicants because we have every confidence in you and we see your potential."

Two months ago, something like that would make me feel proud, sit straighter, smile harder.

Now it makes me feel hollow.

That afternoon, I meet with my future boss, Erica. After my interview six months ago, I followed her on Instagram where we talked about our mutual love of the *Real Housewives*. We chatted after every episode in DMs, but I never thought it would lead to anything.

She told me when I showed up that connecting with her on a human level made me stand out.

But I just really love the *Real Housewives*.

Erica's a frazzled woman who wears her curls slicked back in a ponytail, her skin sallow and the bags under her eyes pronounced. She's draining her coffee cup when I knock on her open door.

I sit down in her chair across from her desk and fold my hands in my lap.

"Hi Isabella, good to see you again. How are you doing?"

"Overwhelmed," I say honestly. "How are you?"

"Exhausted. I had to finish a story this morning and had to get up too early. I haven't watched Bravo in a month, which is a shame." She yawns, and I have a feeling that was an ungodly hour even for a morning person. I don't even want to ask.

"I'm just curious," I say. "Was it really the *Real Housewives* that got me this job?"

Erica shakes her head and laughs.

"Yes and no. We do keep our eye on everyone who gets to the final round and usually hire from that pool if we have a spot open up. I'm not sure what the tipping point was, but the *Real Housewives* wasn't completely it."

She taps a few things on the computer. I try to see what it is, since it's probably a file on me.

"Ah, you wrote a first-hand account of being involved as a hostage in a robbery."

"Yeah, that happened."

Erica places her hand over her chest. "I didn't personally read the article, but the notes in the file say, 'This piece had heart and top-notch reporting.'"

I'm flattered, since I know what I went through to get that story written. I not only lived the story, but took notes on a scrounged-up pad of paper, interviewed Ms. Keller and the police officers involved. While it had the objective angle we need, I added description so the reader could feel what I felt. Like they were there.

It's ironic that was the story that got me noticed.

"Do you enjoy working here?" I ask.

Erica looks surprised. "What do you mean?"

"I mean, do you enjoy working at this paper? Your position."

Erica sits back and crosses her arms. "I've wanted to work at the *Seattle Tribune* since I was a kid. This is the dream."

She sucks down more coffee, and I look around her desk. My gaze falls on her planner. Each day is full of writing, some items crossed out, some highlighted. Post-it notes are everywhere. Her desk resembles mine in Goldheart, just on a much larger scale.

"So, have you found a place to live yet?" Erica asks.

I shake my head. "I'm going to look at apartments tonight."

"Get ready to spend some money."

"Why?" I ask.

"Seattle has become *expensive*. I'm just glad my husband makes good money and we bought our house when we did."

"How expensive?"

Erica waves her hand around. "All of the junior reporters have roommates. Or drive for Uber in their off hours, which isn't a lot. You're here because you love the news, not because you want a good salary."

She laughs and drinks more coffee. "I wouldn't get up at two a.m. if I didn't love the news. I wouldn't not see my husband for anything else."

I watch people outside the window, moving quickly from one end to the other. I pay attention to their energy, whether they carry themselves with happiness. It's something I can't tell from where I am sitting.

"Are you happy?" I ask.

"Happy?" she asks, laughing again. I wonder if she's laughing because she's so tired. "This is what I've wanted since I was a little girl. I've worked my ass off and paid my dues to get here. Of course I'm happy. Of course." She stands up abruptly. "I'm going to get more coffee. Do you want some?"

"No thanks," I say.

"Stay right here and enjoy the stillness. This is the last time you'll be able to relax here."

Erica walks away, and the door floats close.

I lean my elbows onto the desk and drop my head to my hands. What am I doing here?

Erica is lying through her teeth if she thinks she's happy.

The news is my dream too, but I can do it in a town that actually has boundaries, cares about me as a person, and keeps most of their emergencies to business hours.

And she's right about the rent. Rent for a shoebox of an apartment eats about seventy-five percent of my salary, but by the looks of it, I won't have time to spend money, and I'll never be home to enjoy my apartment anyway.

The thought of Goldheart won't leave me alone.

I dreamt about it last night. I tossed and turned, remembering Main Street and how it felt to get coffee at Gold Roast, how the lake is so peaceful in the off-season. I thought the Goldheart residents treated me with skepticism, but they're a hundred times more friendly than folks in Seattle. After the robbery, Goldheart residents started greeting me like I'm a cherished part of the community, not the enemy. So many people asked me how I was, if I was okay, if I needed anything. Someone anonymously paid for ten drinks at Gold Roast for me, just to cheer me up.

Seattle is a wonderful town, but it doesn't feel like *my* town.

It doesn't feel like home.

I'm standing when Erica returns to her office, steam floating from her coffee cup.

"Erica, I have something to tell you," I say.

15

EUGENE

"Who's my best girl?" I ask Bambi, as her paws crunch on the leaves and branches as we walk in the forest. Her snout is to the ground, smelling every scent, her little noises so cute, I could shrivel up now. This morning, she spun in circles in excitement when I put her harness on to go in the truck, and her tail beat the concrete of my garage so hard, I thought she'd break it. She sits in the front seat with me, watching the road like an anxious backseat driver.

I fucking love my dog.

I had to come to the wishing well.

Izzie had been in Seattle for two days. We talked the first night for a couple hours, her yawning more than she talked. She would have to come back here to pack up her apartment, so I decided I would drive her up to Seattle, no matter what our status was at that point.

I have to spend as much time with her as possible, even if we were ending and there would be no more us. I would take her calls whenever she wanted to talk. I would drop everything if she needed me.

I even swallowed my pride and got an iPhone for her. My mother had to teach me how to use all the popular features. She almost downloaded Facebook to my phone, but I put my foot down at that.

Izzie told me about this thing called FaceTime, and that was all I needed. If Izzie was thousands of miles away, I wanted to see her face whenever she would let me.

My boss almost collapsed when I showed it to him. He smacked me on the back and said, "It's the end of an era."

"Hey, I never had a reason to get one before now," I said.

"This girl must be special," Tom said.

Then, something even more shocking happened.

I got a bank account.

If I have to get on a plane, I'd need a card of some kind to book. I don't believe in credit cards, so I refuse to get one, but a debit card is fine. Ms. Keller's eyes bulged when I showed up with all my cash, a pile I collected from all over my house. I know I'll be finding stashes for years to come.

"Wow, what was the change?" she asked.

"You remember Izzie?"

"Oh, that darling girl. Are you two sweet on each other?"

"Yes, ma'am. She changed my mind." I don't mention that she's moving to Seattle, and I need a card since airlines don't take cash.

"Fair enough." There was a glass partition, a new addition

after the robbery. Still, she leaned in to tell me, "I'm proud of you, Eugene."

I love to hear my real name. Because that's what Izzie calls me.

I talked to Izzie this morning, and she was vague on what she was doing today, instead asking me what I was up to. I did mention the walk I'm currently on, and how Bambi and I might make a wish.

Still, I'm shocked when I see a blond head in front of the wishing well, a purse slung over her shoulder.

My heart stops, my cheeks straining with my smile. I don't know if she's a dream or a vision, but I stay still, letting the moment captivate me.

When she turns, I swear she's an angel.

"Hi," she says, clasping her hands in front of me.

"Hi. What are you doing here?"

She smiles through the tears. "I turned down the Seattle job."

Hot damn, miracles do come true.

"You did? What about a bigger market? That's what you wanted."

"It's what I *thought* I wanted," she says. "I had to get away from this town to realize how special it is. How special *you* are."

I take cautious steps toward her. "Izzie, I don't want you making decisions based off of me. I won't let you come back until you know for sure you want this town. I'm just a consolation prize."

"Oh, Eugene," she says. "You're the whole prize. You're the gold-medal ribbon."

"Oh, shucks," I say, touched.

She wipes a tear away from her eye. "I want to see where this goes. I know I'll spend the rest of my life regretting it if I don't give this town, and you, a chance. There's always going to be hustling at bigger papers, and that's not for me. I want to be here. In Goldheart. With you. If you'll have me."

"I will. I definitely will."

Bambi whines, her tail going back and forth at Izzie. My dog is just as keen to love on her as I am.

"Are you excited to see her, Bambi? Are you excited? Go get her!"

I let Bambi's leash go, and she runs toward Izzie, colliding with her legs. She drops down and flops onto her back, presenting her tummy to Izzie.

That says, *I trust you. I feel safe with you.*

I feel the same.

"So?" Izzie asks. "What do you say?"

"Let's do this shit,'" I say, taking her in my arms and kissing her. I lace my hands through her hair as I suck her bottom lip. I set her bottom on the wishing well and kiss her good, holding her against me.

My new ringtone buzzes from my back pocket, and Izzie pulls back, alarmed.

"Is that...?"

"Oh," I say, pulling the sleek phone out of my back pocket. "I got a phone."

"Holy shit," she says, inspecting it. "You'll need a case for it. And a protector for the screen."

"Why do I need that?"

"Those phones break easily."

My eyes bug. "I paid a thousand bucks for this phone, and it's easy to break? What kind of racket do they have going?"

"Why did you get a new phone?"

"I wanted to FaceTime you if you moved. Oh," I say, pulling out my wallet. I show her my debit card. "I also have a checking account now. No more bank trips."

She kisses my cheek. "You don't want to pick up any more girls in bank vaults?"

"Absolutely not. I got the best one. Why should I look for another one?" She kisses my scruff, and I rub it. "I promise I will shave this tonight."

"You better," she says. "I would like sushi. I'll gussy up if you gussy up."

"Eat at the restaurant?" I ask.

"Absolutely," she says. "I want everyone to know out of all of the guys in this town, I got the best one."

"You're so sweet," I say. "I'm definitely treating you not-so-sweet later."

"I look forward to it. We have all the time in the world now."

"Exactly," I say. "Izzie St. Clair is back for good!"

She kisses me and scratches Bambi's head at the same time. "I am."

"Lucky to be with you," I say.

"Lucky to be with you too."

EDITOR'S NOTE

By Isabella St. Clair
Editor-in-Chief

Six months ago, I took the editor-in-chief position at the *Goldheart* Gazette, *not knowing what to expect. Honestly, my plan was to stay for a year, learn as much as I could, and then take that knowledge to a bigger city.*

However, something happened.

I fell in love.

Goldheart is a charming town, born from the dreams of a few men heading west to strike gold. It has held onto that charm, even with modern pressures to change and embrace progress. I love that the majority of shops on Main Street are owned by residents, some with families who can boast over a hundred years of residency here. Although I did not grow up in Goldheart, I was welcomed with open arms and embraced as one of your own.

I do not take that privilege for granted.

From Betty's Café to Gold Roast Coffee, to Ice Dream Ice Cream to Moe's Diner, this town is more than a collection of businesses and residences. It has captured my heart and my love.

I'm committed to you more than ever.

So I welcome your requests and letters. What do you want to see in your paper? What news matters to you? What stories warm your heart and make you feel like Goldheart is the hidden treasure of Placer County? Tell us. Please write into us or fill out a comment card on our website. We would love to hear from you.

And if you allow me to get personal for a moment, I would not understand the beauty of this town without the help of your lifelong residence Eugene "Thumper" Walker. A former MVP from Quartz High School and a member of Holmes Construction, he has shown me the true hospitality that this town has to offer. There's no one else I would rather have been stuck in a bank vault with. No one I would rather share my life with.

I love you, Eugene. And I love this town.

Goldheart, thank you for letting me be your Editor-in-Chief.

LOVE, *Izzie*

WANT MORE?

To keep up to date with Jenny, please go to jennybuntingbooks.com to subscribe to her newsletter!

Loved *Safe with You*? Please consider reviewing on Amazon! It helps others find and enjoy this book.

Thumper first appears in the first Finch family book, *Fool's Gold*, and *Safe with You* overlaps with the second book, *Gold Rush*. Check them out for more Goldheart. *Continue to read the first chapter of* Fool's Gold*!*

If you dig the "stuck" forced proximity, check out my *Stuck in Love* series. It's all romcom novellas where the couple gets "stuck," just like this one. You can purchase them individually in ebook, or as a cute bind-up paperback!

Come find Jenny on socials! She has readers' group on Facebook called Jenny Bunting's Adultish Readers, a Facebook page called Author Jenny Bunting, and she's on Instagram and TikTok at @jennybuntingbooks! She always loves connecting with her readers.

PREVIEW OF FOOL'S GOLD

Chapter One
Cameron

"Emily, the raccoons are back."

I escape inside the sliding glass door and shut it quickly. My sister may be cool with raccoons on her deck, but I doubt she wants one running through the house.

I press my body against the wall, maintaining eye contact with the fatter of the two, currently chowing down on the cat food.

"Go away," I yell at them through the glass. The little fucker keeps eye contact as he dips the dry cat food in water with its creepy hands and stuffs its face.

We don't even have a cat.

My large mug with a C on it sits by a hissing pot of coffee. I pour some liquid gold, trying to ignore the beady eyes and my constant questions of why my sister has sympathy for trash pandas.

The first sip scalds my tongue. "Fuck," I say as I set it down. My eight-year-old niece, Olive, turns the corner into kitchen at the exact time.

"Hi, Olive. You didn't hear that…"

"Hear what?" she asks, pushing her brown hair out of her face.

"Exactly. So, the raccoons are eating the cat food again," I say, pointing as I blow on my coffee.

Distraction is key.

Olive's face lights up. "That's Thelma and Louise."

I blink rapidly. "What?"

"Mommy named them," Olive says, pointing to each raccoon.

"Is Mommy okay with them on the deck?"

Olive shrugs again. She sits in her usual spot, folding her hands like she demands service. That's my cue. I drape a towel over my forearm and walk to Olive's side, doing our usual morning schtick as her mother, my sister, gets ready.

"What can I get you, madam?" I ask in my bad British accent that always makes Olive laugh.

Today, she is stone-faced as she sticks her nose in the air.

"Cheerios, please, with half of a banana."

"Does the lady prefer plain or Honey Nut?"

"Surprise me." Her tiny nose goes higher.

"And what would madam care to drink?"

"Orange juice, please."

"At your service," I say, bowing, and that finally gets a giggle.

I'm glad my back is to her when she says, "Uncle Cam, why was there a lady leaving your house last night?"

Oh fuck. Usually, I get away with it.

There are pluses and minuses to living on my sister's property in my tiny home. It's cheap as hell. Since the structure is paid off, I can live off of very little. I kick in for groceries and electricity, but most of the money I make goes into my bank account. The tiny home is all about freedom—freedom to live the way I want without worrying about money or another person.

The big fat negative is I have to deal with constant judgment from my sister and her daughter about my...habits.

I like women. I like them a lot.

"That wasn't a lady. It was a raccoon," I say, finding the Honey Nut Cheerios and Olive's favorite bowl, a bright pink one.

"Uncle Cam, get real," Olive says.

I wince. I taught her that phrase. Pouring some cashew milk over her cereal and cutting half a banana, I turn and place it in front of her with flair. She puts her elbows on the table to shovel the cereal into her mouth. Emily would usually tell her to get her elbows off the table, but I let it slide.

I pour the orange juice in a plastic goblet Emily used for drunk crawls when she was in college.

My niece uses two hands to drink, and it's the cutest thing ever.

"She's a friend," I say, biting into the other half of the banana.

Olive looks up, her spoon hovering over her cereal. "What's her favorite color?"

"Purple," I blurt out. I have no idea. I'm not even sure of her first name.

"Will she be your girlfriend?" Olive asks.

I choke on the banana piece and cover my mouth to avoid spewing fruit shrapnel.

"I'm content as I am, Martini," I say, using a nickname Emily hates but Olive loves. "I don't want a girlfriend."

"Aren't you getting older?"

Wow, really stick in my gut. I nod. "Yes, I am. Just like you."

"You're *way* older, Uncle Cam."

I swallow again and my neck prickles with heat. "Yes. That is true."

"You need a girlfriend. Get serious," she says, spooning Cheerios into her mouth.

I sip the coffee, but it does nothing for the dry mouth. At our last family dinner, I overheard my sister discussing my love life with my mom. I've lived on my sister's property for seven years, and I've gotten more brazen with the women I've brought home.

"I'm just wondering if he's ever going to grow up," Emily had said to our mother, like the traitor she is. "It was fine when he was in his twenties…"

"Cameron has always been a barrel of fun. He can't be serious. That's the way he is, Emily Jean," my mom had said.

Can't be serious.

That eats at me, like the raccoons chomping on cat kibble.

Emily tears into the kitchen in a panic, ping-ponging from her child to the counter to the fridge, pulling her own brown hair into a ponytail.

"Oh good, she's eating," Emily says. "We have to leave in five minutes."

"You're more anxious than usual," I say, sipping my coffee.

"Dan's coming today," Emily says. She looks me up and down. "We need to stop on the way over there to get coffee and the spread."

"Oh f—," I say, my lips buzzing as I trail off.

"You forgot," Emily says.

"No, of course I didn't."

Yeah, I absolutely forgot.

Emily leans in and sniffs, her nose wrinkling. "Put on a different shirt. Maybe one that doesn't smell like an entire Bath and Body Works store."

"Maybe that's my natural musk," I say as I walk to the sliding glass door. The raccoons are gone. I point to the empty cat dish. "The raccoons are back. Why did you put out cat food? Did you get cat food just for those f—" My lips buzz again as I catch my almost-curse.

I'm getting better.

"Thelma and Louise!" Olive says, lifting her spoon in the air.

"It's fine," Emily says, vibrating with nervous energy.

"I'll be back," I say in my best Arnold Schwarzenegger impression. It always makes Olive giggle, and I see a smile on her face before I turn around.

"Five minutes," Emily yells at me as I take my coffee back to my tiny house.

Ten minutes later, we're in my sister's SUV, the tires crunching on the gravel road. Olive bounces in the backseat, her nose stuck in a book.

"You'll have to tuck and roll, honey," Emily says. Olive barely responds as we pull in front of Goldheart Elementary. The dropoff line is sparse, but Emily barely stops the car before Olive gets out and pulls her backpack onto her shoulders.

"Bye, baby," Emily says with a wave.

"Remember, Olive…" I start.

"Shaken, not stirred," Olive finishes, becoming a different child, swinging her arms and shaking her hips.

Emily glares at me. "I can't believe you."

"What?" I ask as we pull away from the curb. "You're welcome for entertaining your child. Feeding your child. Fighting off the raccoons so they don't tear off the face of your child."

"Raccoons are misunderstood creatures," Emily says. "You're running into Gold Roast."

"What?" I say, the blood draining from my face. My ex-hookup, Tara, owns Gold Roast. She moved to town a few months ago, and I was part of her welcoming committee. Well, my dick was.

After I asked her to leave after acrobatic sex against my ladder, she told me to "eat shit and die" and slammed the door loud enough to awaken the raccoons.

I have sensible reasons for not letting women sleep over. The mattress in the tiny house barely fits me; I'm six-five and I love to do the starfish. Another human can't sleep with me up in my tiny loft bed because I tend to travel. My giant feet would end up in her hair.

I own a tiny home so women don't get ideas. I can't be tamed. After two pseudo-relationships in high school, one that ended with me in the ER with a concussion and a gash on my skull, I haven't dated anyone longer than a week. My dick loves wild women, who usually launch hard items at my head when I inevitably piss them off. Women think they want me as a boyfriend, but I would be the worst. I stopped trying to make things work I'm not good at a long time ago.

Tara didn't tell me she was looking for everlasting love, so I thought it was okay to ask her to leave after we were done.

It was not. I've avoided Gold Roast long enough. Still, my hand hesitates at the door handle.

Emily sniffs out my reluctance like a raccoon finds leftover Chinese.

"Oh God, you slept with her, too? Cam!"

"Blame it on the tequila!"

"Well, time to face the horndog music," Emily says with a point. "That wasn't the woman who I saw leaving your house last night?"

She wasn't, but *fuuuuuucccccccckkkkkk*. Of course I couldn't get that past my way-too-smart sister.

"Why were you up? Your favorite episode of *Law and Order* on again?" I ask.

"I had orders to fill," Emily says, rubbing her face. One of the reasons my sister can afford her beautiful piece of land is because of her kickass jewelry business on Etsy.

Emily shakes her head. "I feel like Dan's going to drop the hammer at any moment."

I roll my eyes. Dan is an angel investor in our family's business, Woody Finch Brewery. Our dad almost bankrupted us, and it would've gone under if it wasn't for Dan Price. With Dan's guidance and investment, we've been able to rebrand, hone our business to build up the brewery experience, and get out of my father's money-pit of a distribution plan.

My dad wanted the glory of being in grocery stores, where the margins are super tight, and neglected the taproom for years. Dan suggested we focus on a taproom model and look at distribution far in the future.

At least, that's what I think he did. I've zoned out at most of the meetings and doodled instead.

Because of Dan, we recently refurbished a barn that had been vacant for some time into a new taproom and are getting decent foot traffic on the weekends. Still, not a lot of people know of us in surrounding areas, and obscurity is our biggest obstacle.

Since our beer is phenomenal.

It finally feels like we're making headway. Dan is ecstatic with us. Still, my sister and mother love to look for worry that's not there.

"Dan is a great guy. He'll understand."

"I hope so," Emily says, gripping the steering wheel.

"Everything's going to be okay," I say. "Relax."

"Oh, thank you so much for that advice. I've never thought of that!" my sister says sarcastically.

My sister needs to take my approach to life. Easy. Carefree. Low stakes.

Emily turns onto Main Street, passing one of many historical landmarks, the church, where prospectors came to pray for a gold mine discovery. Further down the road, Gold Roast Coffee shares space with other small businesses in what used to be the town's bank. Goldheart was founded on California's gold rush, and it's sprinkled with reminders of a time gone by. Lately, the city council's been working on revitalizing the downtown, bringing in tourists and crowding us locals.

Our town refuses to let big-name stores in, so Gold Roast is one of the few coffee options in town. You have to go one town over to get Starbucks, one of the biggest gripes of our tourists. While I see new faces on the street all the time, other Goldheart residents know all about my reputation of drinking at the Swift and bedding as many willing ladies as possible. Jokes are made constantly about me, but I let them slide.

I still wouldn't want to live anywhere else.

We pull into an angled parking spot in front of the coffee shop, and I open the car door. "Your usual?"

"Please," Emily says, smacking her cheeks to wake herself up.

"You got it."

I enter the hallway of the building and duck into the first

door. The air inside Gold Roast is warm and sugar-scented. Three people hover by the pickup counter, studying their phones. I tentatively walk up to the counter to find Tara, my ex-date.

Absolutely pissed to see me.

"Cameron," Tara says.

"Tara," I say, crossing my arms. "I have an order for the brewery to pick up. I think it was paid already. And I need a large almond milk latte, two sugars."

Tara flicks an eyebrow as she stabs the cash register like she wants to stab my eyes.

"That will be eight dollars and six cents."

My eyes bulge. "There's no fucking way."

"That's the price," she says.

I don't know why she's so mad. I was upfront, honest. It's common knowledge I don't do relationships and I just like to have fun. She must've forgotten about the three orgasms I delivered that one night after home-cooked Italian food and some really nice wine.

I don't fight it, pulling out my wallet to find a ten. I hand it to her, and she opens the cash register, placing the bill in and closing it, without counting change.

"Aren't you going to get me my change?" I ask.

"Um...no," Tara says.

I sigh. "It's for my sister, so please don't spit in it," I say as she walks away to make the order.

"Harsh," I hear behind me. Turning around, I find Annie

Stewart, wearing her work's forest green polo shirt and a teasing smile.

The Annie Stewart. Quartz High School's mathlete legend, and my former math tutor. Looking beautiful as always.

We've run into each other over the years, and seeing her is always like finding a twenty you forgot about in your jeans. It puts me in a great mood for the rest of the day.

I also love hugging her every chance I get.

"Hey Annie," I say, opening my arms. Her arms are always strong and comforting around me.

Annie and I have known each other since we were kids. She's six feet tall, so we always got stuck together in the back row of classroom pictures. Her red hair, the color of amber beer, is in a ponytail, and her face is free of makeup.

She looks stunning. But she always does.

When I let her go, I cross my arms. "Were you here this whole time?"

"I saw most of it," she says. "Lovers' quarrel?" She peers around me to look at Tara.

"*Former* lovers' quarrel," I say.

Her malt-colored eyes gleam. "Breaking hearts everywhere like usual, I see, Cam."

"It's what I do."

"What are you up to today?"

"We have a big meeting with our investor this morning. Emily is freaking out," I say, shoving my hands in my pockets.

"I'm sure it will be great," Annie says.

I can't help but grin at that. "Thanks," I reply.

Annie and I have always been friendly, although we had zero in common growing up. She was the yearbook editor and class president, and graduated as valedictorian. I got caught fucking a cheerleader under the bleachers, got ejected from one too many football games for pushing a kid talking shit, and went to summer school every summer to make up for bad grades.

Annie is the only reason I got my diploma. She saved my ass when it was do-or-die for math, and I almost kissed her in the library when I got a C-plus on the final my junior year.

Almost.

We saw each other once and a while senior year, but what little magic we had seemed to have evaporated.

Annie punches me in the arm. "Thank you so much again for setting up Raegan's engagement. I really appreciate it."

"No problem," I say, looking at the ground.

Her sister Raegan and her fiancé Henry came to the first trivia night we hosted at the brewery three months ago. Henry wanted to propose to Raegan through a series of trivia questions about roller coasters and Miley Cyrus, which I thought was weird at first. Then, I heard the story of how they got stuck on a roller coaster during their first date.

Henry proposed to Raegan after dating her for three months.

Stuff like that gives me heart palpitations. I'm not built like that at all. I rarely make it to a third date.

"Annie!" Tara yells from behind the counter.

"Well, it was good seeing you," Annie says, leaving my side. Tara hands her a tray of coffees and a bag. When she passes me, I smell her scent, something tropical with coconut. She turns back and smiles genuinely. "Good luck on your meeting."

"Thanks," I say, as she breezes past me and out the door.

Do not check out her legs, do not check out her legs, sensible me says.

It's such a nice pair of legs, though, horndog me says.

She's the only person who thought I was more than my large dick or athletic ability. I can't ruin her image of me even if I really, really want to stick my dick inside of her.

I'll settle for those sexy-as-fuck hugs.

I breathe as a sigh as Tara slams down the coffee.

"Fuckhead," she says.

"That's me," I say, taking it with a smile.

I watch Annie walk to her Jeep, putting sunglasses on before she climbs in.

Man, whoever she ends up with is some lucky guy.

ACKNOWLEDGMENTS

First, I want to thank Julie Olivia. She not only alpha-read the first few chapters as I wrote them, but designed this beautiful cover. I'm obsessed with it. You are the best author friend a girl can have, and I do not deserve you.

Candice, my sister-in-law, who beta read this novella when complete is everything a girl could want in an in-law. Your feedback helped shape the final product immensely and I'm so thankful for you. You are one of the good ones.

To my editor and proofreader, Lopt & Cropt and Horus Copyediting and Proofreading. You both are the best and it's why I keep coming back.

To my former co-worker Reyna who worked at a bank and confirmed some details I was iffy on. Thank you so much!

I would like to thank Tori Alvarez, the organizer of *A Series of Unfortunate Meet-Cutes* anthology, who was extremely understanding when I pulled out of the project. This novella wouldn't exist in this time and space without the push from your project and I greatly appreciate it.

To my readers—I love you all. Thank you for showing up to every release, for your reviews, for your word-of-mouth, for our chats in messages. I wouldn't do this without you.

ABOUT THE AUTHOR

Jenny Bunting started writing stories as a kid, and romance has always been her favorite. She "published" books by designing construction paper covers and still has a horde of them to this day. It should be noted that Jenny *did* work at a community newspaper. She loves peanut butter, puns, exercise, reading, brunch, and IPAs. Jenny lives with her husband and their German shepherd in the suburbs of Sacramento, California.

www.ingramcontent.com/pod-product-compliance
Lightning Source LLC
Chambersburg PA
CBHW030349180626
46812CB00007B/2816